# CRUCIBLE LUCIFERUM

A.J. CURRY

CROSSROADS OF CROSSTIME

VOLUME IV

RCD PRESS
PORTLAND, OREGON
ROSECITY.DIGITAL

# Table of Contents


**Part 1: Plague Dreams** ........................................ 4

**Part 2: Ellsberg Variations** ........................................ 58

**Part 3: Demiurge, Archangels, & Alien** ........................................ 97

**Part 4: The Crossroad and The Crucible** ........................................ 130

**Epilogue** ........................................ 167

**Afterword** ........................................ 181

**About the Author** ........................................ 183

**About the Publisher** ........................................ 183

**Crucible Luciferum** ........................................ 184

# Part 1: Plague Dreams

## *one: murphy*

“Come to torture me some more?” I asked.

Behind the mask, Dr. Reich laughed with everything but his eyes. “It’s only ‘torture’ because you chose to think of it that way, Mr. Murphy. In any case, I think we can forgo physical therapy today.”

Waking up in a hospital sucks... but there are things that suck worse.

“What’s the point, anyway? You’ve already told me I’ll never walk again.”

“‘Never’ is a long time, Mr. Murphy. People have recovered who were injured worse. But you have to *want* to be healed. Until that happens, there’s only so much we can do for you.”

In the window behind Reich, I could see the skyline of downtown Portland, the air still hazy from the last tear-gassing of the latest protests. Apparently they’d brought me here after the accident I still couldn’t remember and proceeded to save my life–although why anyone had bothered was beyond me.

“In that case, I guess we’re done here, right?”

“Not quite,” Reich said. “Even in your current condition, you’re a threat to yourself and possibly others as well. You have delusions; you act out on them. And apparently, according to your former wife, this has been a problem for some time.”

“You talked to *Caroline*? Is she here??”

“No. We contacted her, of course, since apparently you have no other family. I realize that an estranged former spouse is hardly unbiased in these matters, but she seems to feel you would have benefitted from therapy some time ago–and I tend to agree."

I laughed. It even sounded nasty to me. "Of course you do."

"Whether you think the world is real or not is no concern to me. You certainly aren't the first person who came out of an induced coma with false memories, but yours seem... quite extensive. Most people really don't think anything is real besides themselves, but they learn there are consequences to behaving that way. You haven't–and that's a problem."

"One among many. All I really want is to get out of this place and–no offense–away from you."

"None taken. Getting you 'out of this place' is my first priority as well–but I'm the one who gets to say when and how that happens, Mr. Murphy. Cooperate with me and we'll both get what we want."

"Anyone ever tell you you're a shitty doctor?"

"Frequently."

* * *

Eventually, they *did* let me go–because that's what happens when the insurance runs out, they need the bed, or you learn to keep your contrary opinions to yourself. I still had to see a therapist, though–just not a *physical* therapist.

It had been Dr. Abenard's idea to start keeping a dream journal. "You have these dreams for a reason, Michael. The more you can tell me about them, the better the chance that I can help you find what that reason is."

Her office was conveniently close to the senior's co-op, close enough that I didn't have to call Uber to get there. I like getting around on my own, even in a fucking wheelchair. She was pretty, in an odd and striking way, with enormous dark eyes and dark hair. But I wasn't about to have a crush on my therapist... that ship sailed a long time ago.

"I have dreams for the same reason most people have dreams, Helene. Because reality sucks."

"It sucks for us all, Michael. We're living through a pandemic under a delusional dictator. Our civilization is experiencing the early onset collapse of late stage capitalism while we poison our own planet, while we lose our identities in a plethora of electronic trinkets, toys, and distractions.

"You know it, and I know it... and we're lucky enough to live in a place where it is acceptable to be honest about these things."

"You mean," I said, "At least I'm not still in *Texas*... right?"

"We should stick to therapy, not politics," she replied. "You are *not* 'most people,' Michael, and very few dream as you do–not if the details in your journals are what you truly dream."

I laughed. "I've little enough reason to make this stuff up, Helene. It's not really fun waking up from it and realizing I'm still *here*."

"We all wish that dreams could be real."

"Well, that's the thing–I think they *are* real. I think my mind goes somewhere else when I'm asleep, gets dragged back here when I wake up. I don't believe that my subconscious mind is making this stuff up."

"In your dreams, you are young again and can still walk."

"Not always young. There's other versions of me as well. Sometimes it gets confusing–particularly when they start talking to each other."

"I can see where that might be a problem," Dr. Abenard said. "Do you not also dream of your wife as well?"

"Sometimes," I said. "But even when I do, she's either leaving me or already left. Even in dreams, some things stay the same."

* * *

Getting old sucks, although not as bad as the one known alternative... or maybe not. I was beginning to have my doubts on that score.

There were still some pretty serious holes in my memory. I don't remember the night I drove off the edge of a road into a ravine and almost killed myself, but I remember drinking one hell of a lot after my wife left me, and I don't have much reason to doubt it happened. Something seems weird about the timing, but that's true of a lot of things.

But I've been told the disease I wound up catching in the hospital can have permanent after-effects when it doesn't just kill you. I've also been told that what little I *think* I remember is just an elaborate hallucination from the induced coma that saved my life. Believing that makes more sense than believing anything I think I remember... but it still doesn't *feel* right.

Maybe in some other life I might've been able to retire, but not this one. But I'm lucky enough to have some tech skills that make me useful enough to get to work from home, instead of just sitting in quarantine, waiting for my savings to run out. It gets harder all the time, though, and I'm pretty sure the time is soon at hand that I'll be more or less obsolete.

That's my life: I wake up in the morning from insane fucking dreams, write them down, then put in a long shift writing code for jackass tech bros on a system that tracks my every keystroke and evaluates my 'productivity' down to three decimal points of fictional accuracy. Then I drink–usually at home, unless I can find a bar that isn't under quarantine lockdown. One of these days, the lockdowns will probably just be permanent... along with the plague, along with the tear-gas happy fucking feds, along with the obscene imbecile in the White House who made it all happen.

By which time, I might even be fucking dead.

Once a week, I talk to my therapist about the dreams and stop off at the dispensary on the way home so I can resupply the melatonin-laced CBD edibles that enable me to sleep at all, with or without dreams. I can usually get my food and booze delivered.

The guy I mostly am in my dreams has a more interesting life than I do, but it seems to be awfully complicated. Dr. Abenard thinks I should try my hand at writing fiction, but I have my doubts. Writing code's hard enough... and it's not like I'm getting any younger.

* * *

"Whatever happened to the knapsack?"

"What knapsack, Helene?"

"The one your dream self carried from one side of the world to the other. It seemed to have some importance."

I shrugged. "He probably just left it somewhere. What difference does it make? Even if he were real, he's not real *here*–not him, not his goddam bag. None of it matters... and I don't, either."

"You have these dreams for a reason, Michael. You would be happier, I think, if we could find out why. If you ever dream or recall anything else of this knapsack, you should write it down. And you should certainly tell *me*."

And so it goes.

* * *

Age and despair and loneliness are more crippling than being crippled. I knew the hole Caroline had left in my heart never really healed, just scarred over. Pain that never goes away doesn't stop being pain, although sometimes you stop noticing it. Then you accumulate other pain as well, and you stop noticing that, too. Eventually, you reach the point where your entire life is just one large and complicated strategy for avoiding pain… and you start to wonder if maybe there's not a much simpler way to deal with it.

I wasn't quite ready for the 'early check-out option,' but I found myself considering it more frequently. I even lived in a place where it was *legal*, for fuck's sake. But I'd come to terms with a lot of pain. Up to the point it got worse. I was in no hurry–and also not so sure I wouldn't wake up someplace even worse. Not all of the places in my dreams are an improvement over the waking nightmare of being old, crippled, and alone.

I was thinking about it, in a bemused way, one evening at my favorite local watering hole with decent wheelchair access and a good patio. Earlier that day, I'd gotten my quarterly performance review results from the shitty little Silicon Valley geniuses I wrote code for… and it was not impressive. Having a job was kind of a good thing. My accident and divorce had pretty much used up my retirement savings. Writing code was keeping my mind sharp, actually having something to do kept my boozing to a sustainable minimum.

But I couldn't exactly say I was happy. Or that I had a whole lot of reasons to value my life.

As the waitress walked back to the bar to get me another beer, I found myself momentarily distracted from contemplations of my own mortality. She had an incredibly nice ass, didn't even need heels to get the appropriate amount of sway in her walk. She might've been one of the reasons this was my favorite local watering hole, but strictly as eye candy. As far as anything else was concerned in my life… some other time, some other place.

Still, it was nice to watch. You could almost say that time stood still watching that enchanting little backside headed back to the bar.

Then time *did* stand still. Literally.

The sound of the jukebox and the traffic noise from outside both faded away as I realized little Evelyn's ass was stuck in mid-sway.

"Sorry it took so long, old buddy," said the ghost of Colvin Case. "But they've got you locked down pretty tight. Hacking into your head in the first place was nothing compared to *this* shit."

* * *

Back in my younger days, I'd screwed around with a few drugs. Who hadn't?

More recently, I'd suffered a psychotic break of fairly epic proportions after my wife walked out on me, including some fairly complex induced coma delusions about being some sort of secret agent who could also do magic. All I really know about it is what my doctors tell me. I had also been drinking pretty heavily, which resulted in the accident that had cost me the use of my legs–as well as a lot of my recent memory. I knew that a lot of the things I *thought* I remembered were traces of the delusions I'd suffered, and so were my dreams–or at least that's what my doctors told me.

But they hadn't said one fucking word about having *waking* hallucinations as well.

"Let's just say, for shits and giggles, that I believe you," I said. "And the life I'm living really *is* an induced hallucination. How do I know you aren't part of it?"

"You don't," said the guy I knew wasn't really there. "It's a bit of a problem."

"Speak for yourself. My main problem is that I'm not getting my beer until this hallucination is over."

"On the other hand, you get to ogle your barmaid's ass as long as you like. Cop a feel, if you want to–I sure as hell won't tell. And you might want to consider the possibility that–at least technically speaking... I'm not *really* a hallucination."

I laughed. "The real Colvin Case, the last time I saw him, was a middle-aged mid-manager with a bad comb over and some very spendy tailoring. You, on the other hand, look pretty much the way I remember him as a kid. You may not really be a hallucination... but you aren't exactly real, either."

"The last time you *really* saw 'the real Colvin Case,' not all the comb overs or sharp suits in the world would've done him a lot of good–you just don't remember that right now."

The funny thing was, he really *did* look the way my old running mate and eventual boss looked when the consulting firm I used to work for first hired him... right down to the bad Hawai'ian shirt and worse jeans. And time really was standing still.

"I don't have a lot of time for this," he said. "I had to jack you up to my speed for us to talk at all, and if I do it for more than a second or two in real time, someone is going to notice."

"Someone?" I asked.

"The parties responsible for your current condition. So I gotta make this quick. This sort of thing has happened to you before, you just don't remember it–but you *might*, if you pay attention to your dreams. There's a way out, also. With any luck, you'll remember that, too." He looked past my frozen barmaid to the bar's front door and his eyes narrowed. "Sorry, that's all I have time for. I'll try to check in again later."

I turned to see what he was looking at, but time got unstuck as I turned. I didn't see anything noteworthy.

When I looked back, of course, he was gone.

* * *

Anyone who says they're ready for it... lies.

I must have been asleep, even though I don't remember it. But suddenly all the lights were on, including a few I hadn't known I'd had. A second spasm moved through my body, far worse than the first.

As the pain receded, I realized my arms were being held. Standing over me was a young woman in an emergency medical tech uniform. Part of the blinding light was the one she was shining in my eyes.

The pain was really, really bad.

"Mr. Murphy!" The EMT was probably pretty under the mask, but I was in no condition to notice. Another spasm hit. "Mr. Murphy, we can help you–but you have to help *us*. We need to find your medication. Your housemates said you keep everything in an old backpack in your closet–it's not there. Mr. Murphy–*where's your backpack*?"

Another EMT was unpacking a defibrillator, but I knew it wasn't going to do any good. Behind the med techs, I could see my housemates looking on with appropriate amounts of shock and horror.

Another convulsion hit, and suddenly my legs were working as well–hurting like hell, just like everything else.

"We can make it stop," the EMT said, "but we need your help. *Where's the backpack*?"

I kicked her in the face as the world went black. It wasn't much of a kick... but it did the trick.

* * *

I hadn't really expected to wake up, but I'd expected a hospital if I did.

I was wrong.

The beach was gray, the sky was gray, the water was gray. The dunes behind the beach were topped with dull brown beachgrass that was basically gray as well. The sound of the surf was oddly muted. There were no other sounds at all.

I'd passed out on a few beaches before, but this wasn't one I recognized. Sitting up, I realized I was wearing an old leather jacket I thought I'd thrown away, over a t-shirt, jeans, and boots. After the accident, I'd switched over to sweatpants. They were easy to put on–and who cares what an old cripple looks like, anyway?

I also realized that I wasn't alone. "Here to torture me some more?" I asked.

“I’m supposed to,” said Dr. Abenard. “But I think they’re about to realize this isn’t working and revert to other methods. We need to talk before that happens.”

I realized then that I could stand up... so I did.

Helene Abenard had been recommended as my therapist after the accident that cost me my legs, had been my counselor in all the long, lonely months that I had dreamed of other worlds and other selves while the ‘real me’ slowly died.

And died.

And died again.

“How many times have we been through this?” I asked.

“It really doesn’t matter. And it really doesn’t work that way.” Helene Abenard was a petite woman with enormous dark eyes and dark hair. Only now, the hair was hidden beneath the cowl of a pale grey hooded sweater that paired well with a long skirt the same color as the beach grass. She was also wearing enormous wraparound shades hiding her eyes, shades that seemed hardly necessary in the dim gray light.

“It ‘doesn’t matter’,” I said, “because none of this is real. Including you.”

She smiled sadly. “Oh, ‘Helene Abenard’ is real enough–you might even meet her someday. My own contact with her was brief, but it was enough that I could pretend to be her in a setting I created from your memories.”

“*Very* creative,” I said, “given that I’ve never actually had a therapist.”

“I borrowed her memories of treating someone else. It seemed appropriate.”

“And now I’m... here?”

"This beach is as real a place as anything else is, Michael. At some point, you might even remember it. But that's not important right now."

"What is?" I asked.

"What's important, from my perspective, is that you acquire a broader understanding of the world and the role you are playing. I'm being forced to do certain things, much as an old friend of yours is being compelled as well. He will have soon engineered his own escape. I want you to help me with mine."

"And what do I get?"

"Quite possibly, you get nothing. I have no promises to offer, there are no guarantees I can make–I am, after all, a slave."

If she was an illusion, she was a perfect one. She drew her legs up before her with her arms wrapped around them, resting her head on her knees and gazing at me through those enormous dark shades. I was beginning to realize what she reminded me of.

"Who enslaved you?" I asked.

"I was first made a slave by cousins to the ones that put that mark on your arm. They traded me and my sisters to cousins of your own kind, in hopes of not being murdered by them... but that happened, anyway. Now the murderers are here–seeking more slaves and more murders, starting with yours, if you do not give them what they want."

"Since when does *your* kind have a problem with slavery *or* murder?"

"I see in your mind what you have been told. I see also that you begin to doubt much of it."

"If my mind is that much an open book," I said, "why are we even having this conversation?"

"The parts of your mind you have willed shut remain that way," she replied. "Those who placed the mark of servitude upon you trained you well, altered you in more ways than you know. As for this conversation... the means of my enslavement is not quite so effective as my slaver believes. It is within your ability to end all this. Suffering and pain created what you think of as a 'world,' not unlike the suffering and pain that created *you*. A sacrifice will be required–one that you must knowingly and willingly make."

"Where are we, really? Is this a dream, a simulation, or some sort of parallel universe?"

"An adept such as you should know better than to draw such distinctions. You are where you have always been, Michael–a point of consciousness moving through the infinity of everything that ever has, will, or could exist. Other consciousness greater than either yours or mine shape the unique details of the places we find ourselves. It is only as part of a community of mind that you move through these places at all."

"That may be true of you and your sisters," I said. "But I am not part of a hive-mind. My mind is my own."

The smile grew sadder. "Your mind and body are equally mere loans, dear child. Your cherished individuality is largely an illusion. In time, your kind may find that illusion as limiting as did mine."

"Assuming you do not first harvest us."

"Your instincts and intuitions inform you already that not all you have been told is true. You should trust those instincts."

"I always do."

"There is an intrinsic order to what you think of as 'the multiverse.' What my kind does is a part of that order, but not all creatures understand this. Worlds are not meant to be strung together into a static lattice of empire, an elaborate game of conquest. Neither are they meant to be isolated from the greater whole."

"Worlds? Or universes?"

"Different words and concepts for the same thing," said the creature no longer pretending to be 'Helene Abenard' in what no longer pretended to be a voice. "Everything exists, Michael, and everything exists for a reason. Heed that part of yourself that is part of a greater whole... and you will know what to do."

## *two: ellsberg*

Since it didn't look like anyone else wanted it, I polished off what was left of the coffee. "I thought," I said, "we'd agreed that 'recent developments' were going to be considered 'out of scope'." Since the developments in question were *all* about me... I wanted to know where matters stood.

Helene shrugged. "I cited my non-disclosure agreement *frequently*, Saul, and I suggest you do the same. But all I really accomplished was a failure to confirm or deny." She turned to Admiral Díaz. "I was asked almost *nothing* about our departure from Dayton, which I found odd. They expect to speak to us again, Hiram, and clearly expect more. What do you want us to do?"

We were sitting on a patio in front of the hacienda-style bungalow where we'd been guests since arriving in the Republic of Texas two days before–one of several scattered around a larger building in the same style that was either a headquarters building for the Texas Aircorps or a personal home of General George Washington Bush–or maybe both. Texicans are casual about such things.

A breakfast that had been brought up for us from the main building earlier. It was a pleasant place to sit, but it was already hotter than I care for. All I really wanted was to be back in the Bay Area. Too bad that wasn't happening anytime soon.

Helene Abenard and I are civilian contractors for Republic of California Navy's Bureau of Strategic Intelligence. She's also my therapist–a petite woman with enormous eyes that see *everything*. We aren't spies, exactly, even though that's exactly what *los Estados Unidos de América* was accusing us of being... among other things.

Sitting with us at the table: Admiral Hiram Díaz, the head of Republic of California Navy's Bureau of Strategic Intelligence, and Commander Kayce Cullen–also of BSI and the RCN academy. Also the daughter of my old friend and fellow author of scientific romances, 'Clarke Kimball.' It was too damn bad that she couldn't talk to her dad about the shit we were doing.

On the other hand, she'd probably have to arrest him if she did... same as she'd once arrested me.

Hiram Díaz had engineered that arrest so he could offer me a job. Instead of writing fairly mediocre Sci-Rom as a combination of therapy and supplemental income, I got defense contractor wages for putting the same stuff in top-secret reports.

In both cases, the source material came from my dreams. Then the stuff in my dreams started happening in real life... and things started getting complicated.

At the end of the table, smiling uncertainly at the rest of us, Dr. Ametyst Albion. Formerly a chief scientist at a joint U.S. / California project to study alien technology–sometimes referred to as 'Majestic'–she was now also a BSI contractor, having made a snap decision to defect to California when the opportunity presented itself.

One of the 'crimes' my team had been accused of by the Yanquis was kidnapping her, but the Yanqui presidente accuses *everyone* he dislikes of some crime or other, usually as misdirection from his own crimes. We were also being accused of espionage, even though U.S. 'homeland security' was being remarkably vague about what we were supposed to have been 'spying' on–possibly because we weren't *actually* spies, possibly because the only thing we could have spied on was a project the U.S. and California had kept secret for *decades*.

It raised an interesting question: how much did the Yanquis *really* know about how we'd gotten away from a top-secret conference where every other attendee was currently a 'guest' of the U.S. government? Admiral Díaz had more than a few good reasons to keep that a secret as long as possible, from both the Yanquis and the Texicans... and I had even more good reason, since all evidence seemed to indicate that *I* was somehow responsible.

Or maybe the Texicans already knew. The 'intelligence asset' they were offering to share with us seemed to know just about everything else we were trying to keep secret.

Ametyst's dark, curly, red hair made a nice contrast to the Texas sky–which is just as blue as Texicans say, even if half the things Texicans say qualify as exaggeration. Her abrupt decision to leave with us when we escaped from Patterson Aerodrome was either incredibly impulsive or incredibly brave. Or maybe she was just tired of being lied to and lied about. Yanquis don't exaggerate, they just lie–especially to themselves.

"I basically just answered questions," Ameryst said. "I told them I had met all of you at the Majestic Conference, that I had been unhappy with my work for a long time, and that what looked like a military lockdown we were able to evade made me decide to leave. I told them I was with you when you found a way out of the conference auditorium, stayed with you… and left."

Hiram Díaz is a big man, built like a brick, with olive skin and gray, wavy hair. I don't trust him any further than the very short distance I could throw him, but he's earned my respect, particularly after the events of the last week or so. He was about to earn some more respect–or maybe throw it all away.

Díaz perched his antique gold-rimmed reading glasses atop the wavy hair and rubbed his eyes. It looked like the accumulated fatigue of the last two days might finally be catching up to him. "Thank you, Dr. Albion," he said. "I appreciate your discretion.

"Helene, matters are not so simple as me telling you what *I* wish you to do. I am but one member of the Admiralty Council, which is *not* of one mind on the current crisis. Until I have their clear direction, we must tread carefully here."

* * *

Two days before, the previously secret proceedings of the annual 'Majestic Conference' at Patterson Aerodrome had become considerably *less* secret when my team narrowly evaded being detained with the other conference attendees, by heavily armed men claiming to be members of the "United States Space Force."

Of course, *los Estados Unidos de América* has no such thing... at least in *this* universe.

The reason we weren't detained was because, when the leader of 'Space Force' took the stage to announce that he was firmly committed to the Yanqui Presidente's vision of 'making America great again,' he was accompanied by one of the things I've had nightmares about as long as I can remember–only this time, *I* wasn't the one screaming in pain.

Not an actual scream, of course. I don't think they *have* voices. But the scream in my mind was far worse. Then something happened that I don't really understand... but at some point, I'm going to have to explain it, anyway. One second we were all in a locked and guarded auditorium; the next second we were kilometers away–in a hotel ballroom, where a defense contractor was holding a dance party as part of the annual 'Dayton Exposition and Air Show' that serves as a cover story for the Majestic Conference.

This particular defense contractor turned out to be an old friend of Admiral Díaz: General George Washington Bush of the Texas Air Corps–'G.W.' to his friends–who had come to the airshow to sell jet aircraft and party... and had more or less run out of jets.

With General Bush's help, we'd gotten back to the airship docks, managed to lift out of Dayton, and were headed back to the Republic of California when a confrontation with U.S.A.F. attack craft steered us into Texas instead.

Most of this I found out after the fact–I spent most of the trip to Texas strapped down in *RCN Morrison's* infirmary, recovering from whatever had actually happened when I saw that... *thing* on an auditorium stage.

And having more dreams.

It wasn't until we were on the ground in Texas that I started to feel like myself again–just in time to find out my entire team had been charged with espionage and kidnapping by the deranged Yanqui Presidente. While I was working my way through that, I found out that General Bush wanted to introduce me to yet *another* damned alien.

After the last year of my life, that wasn't nearly as surprising as it might've been. After you find out that one rumored alien spaceship crash in Texas turns out to have been literally true, it's not that hard to believe in another. At least the Texicans had managed to keep *this* spaceship to themselves. They had also made far better progress with restoring/reverse engineering the wreckage, even restoring the pilot in the process... Well, more or less.

In contrast, the wrecked 'mystery disk' the U.S. Air Force had commandeered from the Republic of Texas was almost as much a mystery now as it had been when it crashed–even after an agreement with the Republic of California brought in some *real* scientific talent.

A mystery that, quite possibly, no longer mattered.

* * *

"Helene, Dr. Albion, I must ask if you were pressed for details on our departure from the conference. I also need to know when, *exactly*, you found it necessary to claim 'non-disclosure' privilege. I fear it is only a matter of time before such privilege yields to larger concerns."

Helene spoke first. "I was mostly asked about my research for BSI. There were questions about my treatment of Saul, but I cited client/therapist privilege in all cases. I told them that I would require either Saul's written permission or a court order to say anything further. However, I *did* tell them that I had not treated Saul prior to his own involvement with BSI.

"The question of our departure from the Majestic Conference and Dayton Aerodrome did not come up at all."

"I wasn't asked about it, either," Ametyst said. "And that's *technically* the only thing that would've been covered by my own NDA."

I hadn't known Ameryst was already under a non-disclosure agreement, but I wasn't surprised. I also wasn't surprised that Hiram had back-dated it to cover the 'recent events' he'd asked us to not talk about immediately before arriving in Texas.

When they got around to questioning me… the NDA wasn't going to help at all.

Díaz sighed. "When we arrived here, I directed you all to assume we would be under constant surveillance. Even though that remains a possibility… I am going to speak as plainly to you all as possible."

"Is that wise, sir?" Kayce interjected. Tough, smart, and insanely loyal to her friends and family, Kayce Cullen was as close to a friend as I currently had. As compact and blonde as Díaz was large and dark, I knew she was just as tough, if not tougher. Whether or not it was a good idea… I also trusted her.

So did Díaz. "Possibly not, Commander. But we have a short amount of time, and I need to ensure that we are not miscommunicating in an effort to not 'confirm or deny' information our hosts very likely already have.

"I have agreed to a second round of interviews, this time with members of Texas Department of Public Safety's Special Operations group. They will be interviewing me as well."

"Am I included in this also?" Kayce asked.

"No, Commander, although you will be joining us at the main building as well."

"Joining for what?"

"The admiralty is, shall we say, *skeptical* of what I have felt free to discuss over a secure comms channel that could still be tapped at the source. I do not believe they would be any less skeptical, were I to speak more freely... *quite* the contrary.

"They wish to speak to *you*, Kayce–they wish to do so as soon as possible."

"*In person*?"

Díaz smiled a wry smile. "If that was considered an available option, the Texicans would be strapping me into a rocket plane this very minute.

"No, you will be using the same teleconference equipment I have been using–the only difference is that I *strongly* suggest you change into a dress uniform before doing so."

"Admiral, what should I *say*?"

"You will answer their questions, Commander. I cannot instruct you in this, but I *will* ask you to be mindful of the magnitude of recent events. The admiralty needs to understand that we have *every* reason to believe the Yanquis have formed a dangerous alliance with an unknown power–and that they have apparently abrogated the terms of the Majestic Agreement.

"Until we know more about this 'space force' and their *true* intentions, I feel that we have no other choice than to assume that they are potentially hostile to California interests–but that is *my* view, and I do not believe my fellow admirals expect your *strategic* analysis. I think they are trying to verify, if possible, what I have already told them."

“What if my answers don’t line up with yours?” Kayce asked.

“If our answers were the same, they would be assumed to be rehearsed and would not be trusted–my fellow admirals are not fools. The call is scheduled in two hours. I suggest you make yourself ready.”

“What about me?” I asked. “Does anyone need to be talking to *me*?”

“Considering your–shall we say, ‘unique’–role in recent events, I am not at all certain *who* should be talking to you, Sr. Ellsberg. Please remain here for now. Once Commander Cullen has conferred with the Admiralty… I suspect things will move *quickly*.”

[[Major Kuehng (don’t forget the umlaut)]]

“Admiral, what should I *say*?”

### three: murphy

When I woke up, instincts I hadn’t always had made me lay still with eyes shut while I used hearing and other senses to try to figure out where I was.

“I *know* you’re awake,” Wolfeich said. “Care for a drink?”

It was beginning to come back to me. And a drink didn’t sound bad.

I opened my eyes. I was laying on a cot. A faint whirring I’d heard when I woke up turned out to be a small ceiling fan hanging over me from the framework of some sort of tent. I swung my feet to the floor and sat up. I realized I was still wearing the same white linen pants I had been given on my arrival. A matching shirt was folded on the ground next to the cot, replacing the one that had been ruined during my interrogation. Sitting next to it, the black leather belt I’d also been given when I’d arrived–but no Moon Knife in the ornamental scabbard… not surprisingly.

A few feet away, Colonel John Carter Wolfeich sat in a camp chair next to a small table bearing a wine bottle and a glass, sipping from a glass of his own. He was still wearing the black tactical field pants and jackboots he'd worn on arrival, but had ditched the tunic. The white undershirt wasn't much different from any t-shirt I'd seen on any other world. He was big the way I used to be big, the first time I was young. He had humorless gray eyes, short dark hair, shaved high on the sides... and a mustache that didn't quite conceal what looked like a memento from a knife fight.

"Certain assumptions were made about you upon our arrival, sir, that I no longer believe are true. I'd like to apologize for that–I *always* believe that it's possible to make amends. This is a fairly good local tempranillo, if you appreciate such things." He gestured to another camp chair next to the table. "Please be my guest."

"Beer's better," I said, putting on the shirt and clasping the belt around my waist. "But sure."

He had an interesting accent–southern, for the most part, but pronouncing some words in a way that sounded almost 'English' back where I come from.

Which could mean almost anything... back where *he* came from.

Joining him in the other camp chair revealed the rest of the tent to me... including something I probably should've expected to be there. But it still surprised me.

"If that's the fuck what I think it is," I said, "what the fuck is it doing *here*?"

"That, sir, is a Moon wog–*my* wog. And I rather suspect... you already *know* what it's been doing here. Congratulations, by the way. No one, to my knowledge, has ever resisted that particular form of interrogation."

“Let’s just say it’s not my first rodeo,” I said, draining the offered glass of wine, holding it out for a refill. “Why’s it strung up in a tube like that?”

At the far end of the tent, past the cot I’d woke up in, was a crystal tube, maybe a yard across and two high, full of a clear fluid that I highly doubted was water.

Floating in the fluid was one of the creatures I’d learned to call ‘Greys’ a lifetime ago, ‘Selenites’ more recently. Even though they all look the same... this one seemed oddly familiar. The enormous and unblinking black eyes did not focus on anything–but I felt the thing’s gaze, nonetheless.

Cables ran from the creature’s skull to the top of the top. Another cable ran from the top of the tube to some sort of console sitting a few feet away on a folding table. Some of this hardware looked... strangely familiar.

“A necessary precaution,” Wolfeich said. “They are dangerous until you domesticate them, then they’re useful. But they have a tendency to die separated from the hive. This preserves them.”

“I’ve heard them called a few things, but ‘wog’s’ a new one on me.”

“*Pseudohominus lunae,* if you want the scientific name,” Wolfeich said. “I expect your people call ’em something different. To me... it’s just a wog.”

A few pieces at a time, it was beginning to come together.

I’d been on a mission, I’d been taken captive. That mission had started out in a world and a life almost as bleak as the induced nightmare the ‘wog’ had used to torture me... and eventually led me here, in a world that wasn’t even supposed to be exist.

Along the way, I’d been made young again by the inhuman bastards I work for–in exchange for some fairly high ‘return on investment’ expectations. I'd also been given cybernetic enhancements any porn or gaming enthusiast would pay a fortune for... but I would *highly* recommend working on the antivirus software before taking this shit to market. The sentient computer virus I'd picked up along the way would be pretty intolerable... if I couldn't turn the son of a bitch off.

I'd been made faster, stronger, etc., with improved ability to recover from physical damage–although I hadn't really known about *that* part of the bargain until Wolfeich's men had worked me over. Not getting what they wanted, they'd then resorted to a more subtle form of 'enhanced interrogation.'

Decades before, I'd undergone similar psychic torture–not so much for information, more to immobilize me... as well as for kicks, if I was to believe what I was later told. I'd gotten through that as well, broke out of it pretty much the same way: an imagined act of homicide/suicide.

Shooting the hallucinatory ghost image of my former wife in the face to break out of a torture loop was a memory I could do without... but I've gotten used to it. Kicking an EMT in the face to ensure my own death–dying alone and lonely, a bitter and broken old man, at the end of a failed and broken life... I guess I'll get used to *that* false memory as well, at some point. Maybe I'll even get used to the memory of it happening *repeatedly* in an endless loop of emptiness and despair...

Just not right now.

"It's an *adequate* tempranillo," I said. "But if you are trying to make amends for what your 'wog' did to me, this doesn't even come close. I'm assuming there's a reason I'm not in a back room getting a few more ribs cracked."

"Indeed there is, sir–the reason is that I am neither a fool nor a sadist. If you interrogate a man long enough, he'll say *anything*... and it might even be true or useful. Or it could be a complete fabrication. And under present circumstances, I'm in a poor position to verify much of anything."

"What circumstances are those?"

"Perhaps little different from your own," Wolfeich said. "When I found this little jungle compound, I took you and your–sisters, wives, whatever they are–I took you to be something I'd seen before, based upon appearances. Half-caste Barsoomians, to be specific. I'm still inclined to think as much of the other two–although they seem *quite* degenerate, even by the standards of Barsoom. Not so yourself, sir. I think you are from someplace different."

"And what if I am? What difference does it make?"

"Perhaps no difference at all, perhaps *all* the difference. You may be just as stranded here as I am, in which case tryin' to beat information out of you isn't much more than just giving my men something to do.

"On the other hand, you just *might* be from someplace a lot further away than just another planet. You *might* have gotten here as I did, or you might've gotten here some other way altogether–your looks rather argue against that, though. I have a hard time believing that a man turning up looking just like a Barsoom creole is mere coincidence."

It probably wasn't... not if 'Barsoom' meant anything in Wolfeich's native timeline, close to what it meant in mine.

I took a long sip of wine and a long look at the 'wog' as I considered my words. I'd never been this close to one of these things that wasn't either a pickled corpse or something I was busy turning into a corpse. Seeing a live one right now wasn't anything I'd expected... even though I'd sort of expected the little grey bastards were going to turn up at *some* point.

I would probably still be getting mindfucked by this one, if a digital ghost hadn't hacked his way into the torture illusion and put the seed of doubt in my mind. It had been too perfect, that illusion. This creature was entirely too intimately aware of every pain or doubt I'd ever experienced, knew all too well the life I had led before my rebirth–had *perfectly* crafted the illusion of a life even more bitter and bleak than the one I'd been reborn from.

Or perhaps it had found, in the infinite reaches of the multiverse, a perfect alternate version of my life that it could use to torture me–if what the thing had said to me at the end of my torture was true. If what else it had said was also true, this creature was a slave... and likely being tortured as well.

The great black eyes seemed unseeing, but that made no difference. These creatures had other senses than sight. In another universe, a man who had once been my friend was being mutated into an abomination... solely to cultivate those same senses.

And he was also being tortured. Tortured to the point that he had cloned an image of himself into the implants in my brain, just for some semblance of an escape. Given that *he* was the one who had first psychically tortured me... my sympathies were somewhat limited.

Was there anything in all the universes except disappointment, torment, and pain? Illusions, lies, and torture? Vain efforts at escape?

Wolfeich had tortured me, tortured this thing in the tube, compelled it to torture me as well. But for all I knew, he was just another escapee, fleeing from some unique pain of his own.

Not that it mattered.

“There are no ‘mere coincidences’, Colonel,” I said. “Not in any of the worlds I’ve known, not in whatever world made you.

“Maybe I’m ‘stranded,’ maybe I’m not. Maybe I’m what you call a ‘Barsoom creole’... or maybe not.

“Or maybe the world isn’t really what either one of us were told, by creatures we *both* should have known better than to take at their word.

“You want to make ‘amends?’ We can talk. But let’s start with this one clear understanding: you are in well over your head... ‘sir.’ And I may or may not be how you get out from under the shit show you’ve dug yourself and your command into–but whatever I have to offer can’t be beaten or mindfucked out of me. You’re going to have to ask–and I suggest you get used to saying ‘pretty please.’

“Any questions?”

## four: kayce

There was a full-length mirror mounted on the wall outside the teleconference suite, for fairly obvious reasons. The person who looked back at me from the mirror was more or less who I expected to see. My hair was grown out a little further than the buzz cut I prefer, and darkened a little bit past the bleached tint my wife prefers. My dress blues were a little snugger than I like–probably because I hadn’t been to the gym in over a week, and had been drinking with the likes of Hiram Díaz and George Washington Bush.

Plainly, I needed to get back to my better habits as soon as possible.

A technician in a gray jumpsuit had met me at the comms center and led me back to the conference suite. He unlocked the door and handed me a piece of paper with a string of handwritten numbers and letters.

“What’s this?” I asked.

“That’s the encryption code we were waiting for,” the tech said. “You got five minutes to connect. If you can’t secure the connection before the code expires, we’ll need to reschedule and get a new code.”

“Sounds like I’d better hustle.”

“You’ll be fine,” the tech said, closing the door behind me.

He was right.

* * *

“Our thanks, Commander Cullen,” said the woman seated in the center of the screen. “We appreciate your availability under these circumstances.”

“But of course, sir,” I said. “I am here to provide whatever the admiralty council requires.”

It was *not* the entire council. I faced Admiral Janice Castillo, Admiral Noah Kahananui, and Admiral Naomi Adeoye. Even so, I was in a meeting with the supreme command of roughly half the operational forces of the California Navy… who plainly wanted a second opinion on whatever my *jefe* had told them.

No pressure… much.

“Our requirements are less than you might think, Commander,” Admiral Castillo continued. She had gray hair, cropped almost as close as I preferred mine, and blue-green eyes that reminded me of the color of the

Pacific. Appropriate, I suppose, for an admiral. She was smiling… but it was not a kind smile.

“Before we continue,” she said, “I must ask a question. Admiral Díaz has implied that he feels the facility you are speaking from may not be entirely secure. Do you have any thoughts on this?”

For a moment, I considered the handwritten encryption key I'd been given on my way in… and what it implied. Then I answered. “I typically rely upon Admiral Díaz's knowledge in these matters, given that it is not my field of expertise.”

“We have *all* relied on Hiram's expertise in such things,” said Admiral Kahananui. “Understandably–were it not for his efforts, I fear RCN would be at a dangerous disadvantage. But that reliance makes him a unique conduit and what engineers might refer to as a ‘single point of failure.’

“For purposes of this conversation, we are directing you to ignore that judgment. You are to assume this communication channel is *completely* secure and that you are free to speak. Is that understood?”

“Yes, sir,” I replied.

“Let us be clear,” said Admiral Adeoye. “You are here neither to contradict or confirm information we've received from your commanding officer. That would be *inappropriate*, outside of actual legal proceedings. We merely need you to answer questions. On the basis of those answers, the full admiralty council has empowered us to make a determination and provide orders that will expedite your team's next steps. Is this also understood?”

“Yes, sir.”

“Very good, Commander. Let us proceed.

"In your own words, as best as you can recall, can you please provide an overview of the events occurring between the *Morrison's* departure from San Francisco and its arrival in San Antonio?"

## *five: murphy*

From where I was sitting, high in a tall tree just inside the timberwork boundary of *La Comuna de las Hermanas*, I could see the ancient pyramid where a fallen angel had once performed an act of unspeakably powerful ceremonial magick. Past it, at the far end of the compound, I could see a vehicle that I might've once called a 'ghost airship' moored to another tall tree. Either this craft, or one very like it, had followed me all the way from Oregon to Guatemala–or maybe had just turned up at opportune moments. I didn't know enough to have an opinion.

I felt fairly sure that I could leap from this tree, clear the timberwork wall, and disappear into the rainforest surrounding this place. I was also fairly sure that the other side of the wall was being patrolled by Wolfeich's men, who may or may not be under orders to vaporize me if I tried any such thing. The truce I'd negotiated with their boss had gotten me another bottle of fairly adequate local tempranillo, but I had no reason to believe his generosity was going to extend much further than that... starting with the fact that the son of a bitch was crazy.

Then again, I was sitting in a tree getting shithammered in preparation for talking to a guy who wasn't really there. Sometimes 'crazy' is a relative proposition.

In the compound below me, I could see various members of *La Comuna* going about their daily business under the watchful eyes of various members of the 'Barsoom Expeditionary Force.' Wolfeich and his men no more belonged in this universe than I did; the 'Earth' they'd come from might've had a few advances over the one I'd started in, or maybe just a couple of lucky breaks. They had space travel and rayguns, but the rayguns and the 'spaceship' looked like stolen tech–may be stolen from the same source as the tech used to control a Grey alien as a slave... tech that looked strangely familiar.

The rest of their gear looked pretty much like the same stuff where I come from. Stolen or not, though... those rayguns were *scary* effective.

That said, the women of *La Comuna* had some fairly scary abilities of their own, at least the elder sisters. They were obviously permitting themselves to be held hostage, for reasons they were probably not going to share with me. The eldest of them all, the immortal Astarte, was under even closer guard–although the guards had no idea what they were *really* guarding.

I slugged down more wine, decided it was time.

Touching my index finger to a hidden contact point behind my ear, I muttered "activate social interface." It didn't have to be loud, but I couldn't just *think* it–it doesn't work that way.

A staticky blur swept across my vision and condensed onto another tree branch, outward and upward from where I sat with my back against the tree trunk. The blur resolved into the digital ghost of Colvin Case. The branch could not have supported his weight if he was real, but the illusion he was painting on the alien hardware in my head was otherwise perfect– a replica of who he'd once been, decades and universes away from this place: a big blond kid with a midwest accent and a mullet, dressed in Adidas, shitty mom jeans, and a worse Hawai'ian shirt.

Back then, we'd been the same plausible fiction–'digital asset consultants' working for the Southern U.S. branch office of an unnamed 'consulting company' with headquarters somewhere in the suburbs of Washington, D.C.

As a guy working in the 'hardware' side of the business, it was equally plausible for me to be gone for days and weeks at a time, doing 'on-site consulting' in places I tended to not talk about.

And since all a lie ever needs to be is 'plausible'... it worked.

The plausible fiction of Case's life ended that day. The plausible fiction of my own life had ended months before when the woman I'd lied to for years finally left me. The fiction of Case being my friend ended with him psychically torturing/immobilizing me with the memory of her leaving... on an endless fucking loop.

Until I found a way to break the loop. And end Case's mission.

After Case's mission failed, I got to go back to the plausible fiction of being a *retired* 'digital asset consultant.' Case wasn't so lucky. The inhuman bastards I work for had a use for him. By the time I saw him again, decades later, he'd been mutated into a marginally human lab experiment that didn't look particularly human... except for the eyes.

But he was human enough to feel pain, human enough to be desperate, desperate enough to settle for a vicarious escape–the escape of loading a digital copy of himself into the hardware in my head.

I hadn't been too happy about it when I found out, but digital ghost Case had managed to make himself useful–and, at some point, I began to remember why the *original* Colvin Case had once been my friend.

I was willing to give Ghost Case a pass on the whole 'torture' thing. The residual psychic link it had left was the main reason I'd been offered this mission in the first place. Also, according to Ghost Case, the original Case–let's call him 'Case Prime'–had been under mind control at the time.

Working with Ghost Case reminded me a *lot* of the 'good old days' when Case Prime had been front office and I had been field operations for one of The Company's more notorious 'dirty tricks' units. Concealing my double agent status had been pretty simple, back then.

Back then, The Order–the inhuman bastards I *really* work for–rarely asked me for much more than information. Had it not been for a cosmic accident that made Case Prime's 'people' decide to activate him, we probably could've taken the secret of our respective extra-human alliances to our respective graves.

If I did not play the present situation with appropriate finesse... we would both wind up in the *same* grave.

"I was wondering when you were going to check in," Ghost Case said. "Or *if* you were going to."

"I can't activate the hardware with my hands tied," I told him. "It's a design flaw I should probably take up with The Order, if I ever see them again. I've been incapacitated in other ways as well–and even though I don't trust all of my memories of the experience, it seems like you should know something about it."

"Yeah, you could say that. It might even be safe to say you owe me... if I was really here."

"If you were *really* here," I told him, "I'd say we were even, at best. But you're not. Tell me what I need to know, and I'll consider myself indebted to a sentient computer virus."

"Indebted enough to level with me? There's a lot of things you've been keeping to yourself, old buddy."

"With good reason that may or may not still apply. I'll *consider* it. But you first."

"I'll tell you what I can, but first–I gotta ask: is *that*," he nodded toward the craft tethered to a tree on the other side of the compound. "Is that what I think it is?"

"I'd say it's *exactly* what you think it is, even though I'm still piecing together the details. You want to know more? How about you tell me how you busted me out of... whatever the hell that was."

"'Hell' is as good a word for it as anything else, old buddy–and you had to bust *yourself* out. All I could do was show you the door."

"Which was hard enough, from what I remember."

"You were locked down, dude. It's the same thing Real Me did to you once, only *she's* a helluva lot better at it than Real Me ever was."

"She?"

"You know who I'm talking about," Case said.

"I suppose so," I told him, "but I still want to hear you say it."

The 'social interface' of my implants had been switched off since long before Wolfeich and his soldiers arrived. There was no way Case could know that the 'Barsoom Expeditionary Force' had arrived with a Grey alien in tow unless he had either lied about having direct access to my mind... or had other abilities he hadn't bothered to tell me about.

Either way, I had to know.

"She wasn't here when we first got here," Case said. "But there is at least one Grey here now. I can sense her; she *might* be able to sense me."

"*How*? Because the original version of you is partly one of them?"

"My mind is a copy of his mind, and I have at least some access to all six of your senses. But if you're worried about me being able to get into your mind, don't be... I can't do that.

"But–in case you haven't noticed–your 'rejuvenation' means you now have more raw psychic ability than you've ever had before. If your mind was built more like mine... you could probably sense her as well."

"No offense," I said. "But I'll pass."

"None taken," he replied. "Just be glad it worked. Even with 'social interface' switched off, I *knew* you were being attacked. I knew it, because Real Me once did the same thing. I didn't access *your* mind, Murphy... I got into *hers*. I was able to infiltrate the illusion for just under a second–but that was enough."

"Yeah, it was," I shuddered at the recollection. "And yeah, I guess I do owe you."

"Not just me, old buddy."

"What do you mean?"

"What I mean is that she *let* me do it–you owe her as well."

I sighed. "Yeah, I guess I do."

## *six: ellsberg*

No matter how much Díaz tried to downplay it, the fact that Kayce was taking his place in the call to the admiralty clearly bothered him. Everything I know about military protocol I learned from working for BSI. The first thing I'd learned was that *nobody* in California Navy operated the way Hiram Díaz did. Guys who win by bucking the rules don't get a lot of sympathy from folks that win by playing it safe... particularly after their luck runs out.

In the flat distance past the Texas Air Corps aerodrome, I could see the adjoining field for commercial air traffic. Part of me was perversely tempted to see just how far I would get if I tried to walk that distance and catch a flight back to Frisco. Probably not very far, and it was turning into yet another broiling hot day. Instead, I amused myself with the televisor and the newspapers. If anyone wanted me, they knew how to find me.

I also wondered how, exactly, I was going to recount the last week of my life to whoever wound up interrogating me–or even the last *year*, for that matter. Living in the bubble of Díaz's task force, I'd gotten used to being surrounded by people who accepted at face value that I had been fed dreams for years by non-human actors who were now reaching through me to manipulate things in the waking world.

How was I going to explain to any rational human being that non-humans had reached out through me to move a crippled airship from one side of a mountain to the other? Or that the shock of seeing one of those same non-humans, psychically screaming in pain, had caused me and four other people to move instantly from a locked auditorium to a hotel ballroom several kilometers away?

How was I going to explain that my dreams now included a running dialog with someone who apparently had 'alien' problems of his own? Or that my waking reality now included being introduced to *yet* another alien? 'Ruhl Skattersmythe' was unlike anything I had ever seen before, dreaming or awake, but he confirmed that I was, as he put it, 'infected with dreams' from otherworldly sources. And he clearly knew that more was happening than mere dreams.

But Ruhl himself was like a dream from an otherworldly source, hinting at cosmic secrets spanning universes. If *half* the things he had told us were even *half* true... the world I'd thought I lived in was even more of an illusion than I'd thought.

Which might not be a bad thing, actually.

The televisor and the newspapers only depressed me. The insane babbling of the Yanqui presidente reminded me of something from my dreams–the same dreams where I see cities incinerated and continents laid to waste by floods, fires, and blizzards.

I brewed another pot of mediocre Texican coffee and tried to distract myself with a crossword puzzle. It was nice having a puzzle I had a modest chance of solving. I'd considered spiking the coffee with some rum I'd found in the guest house kitchen... but only briefly. I needed to be sharp, whatever happened next.

It was a relief when my phone finally rang. "Ellsberg," I said.

"Apologies, Sr. Ellsberg," came the voice of Hiram Díaz. "For not calling you earlier. I felt you would be more comfortable where you are, saw no need to disturb you."

"That's appreciated, admiral."

"You are needed **now**. A car is being dispatched. Please be ready when it arrives."

* * *

When I arrived at the main building, my driver handed me off to an orderly who walked me back to a conference room, opened the door for me, then left–closing the door behind them.

Seated around the long conference table were people I knew... and people I didn't. On the left, my team: Admiral Díaz, then Kayce–both in uniform–then Helene, and lastly Ameryst–still smiling nervously under her flame-red locks. The seat next to her was clearly intended for me, and I took it.

Seated at the head of the opposite side of the table was General Bush, wearing his characteristic smirk and what I guessed was his actual uniform for a change–a short gray jacket, gray pants with blue side stripes, a dark shirt, and a bolo tie. Next to him: a tall woman with graying shoulder-length hair wearing a corduroy blazer over a dark shirt and pants.

Next to her: a big man with a broad face under a Texican-style vaquero hat with the brim tightly rolled to either side of his face, wearing a gray flight jacket over black combat fatigues. Next to him: a slightly built younger man with short, curly, bleached hair and brown skin, wearing thick-rimmed glasses, and a rumpled suit.

"Alrighty, then," Bush said. "Glad you could join us, Mr. Ellsberg. Sorry to keep you waitin' all morning, but there were some things we had to get straight. There's also more than a few things we're hoping you can help us figure out.

"Now that the *entire* team is here... let's get this party started."

## seven: murphy

"All I really know," I said, "is they're not from around here either."

I'd finished off the tempranillo. Another bottle would've been nice, but climbing down a rainforest tree in the dark after polishing off a couple of bottles of wine and a bit of brandy was probably pushing even *my* luck. Regardless, it was my turn: Case had told me what I wanted to know.

Unfortunately, I even believed him–which was about to make things complicated.

"So *another* accessible parallel Earth just got added to the list?" Case said. "How many are we up to?"

"At this point, I'm only keeping track of the ones shooting at me. When Evangeia's people first initiated me, there were maybe half a dozen crosstime-capable species operating on my Earth. They'd evolved on versions of Earth separated by millions of years of probability space–maybe billions, when you factor in the Greys.

"The only reason you and I are even here is because the number of 'Earths' started going up, the gaps started getting smaller, and the people I work for started getting worried. I'm pretty sure the key divergence between this Earth and mine happened about 500 years ago local time... when Astarte closed all the wormholes and told the multiverse to fuck off.

"Even though it sounds like he took the scenic route to get here, Wolfreich started out on an 'Earth' maybe even closer than mine–close enough to have a 'United States,' far enough away to have either developed or stolen some... fairly interesting technology.

"On the trip down here from Oregon, I tried to keep up on the news, but it just got too damned weird. Half the stuff showing up in 'UFO reports' looks like stuff I remember from my Earth, but half of it is *totally* weird. I think whatever Astarte did to seal off this world isn't just coming undone, I think it *backfired*.

"The Fortuned think the 'walls between worlds' are thinning, and it scares them. How do you maintain a stable interdimensional empire–or a stable *anything*–if the entire multiverse, or even just the local piece of it, collapses into chaos?

"They don't know why it's happening, but I think I do. I think what happened on this Earth *caused* it."

I still had major misgivings about trusting him, but Case was right about me owing him. If it wasn't for him, I would still be 'dying' repeatedly in a nightmare version of my own past–as many times as it took for Wolfeich's 'wog' to get what Wolfeich wanted.

"Then 'Barsoomians' are the same as the Fortuned?" Case asked.

"Either the same inhuman bastards or close enough. They never bothered to colonize Mars in my universe–who in their right fucking mind would? Maybe the 'Mars' in Wolfreich's home universe is better real estate... who knows?

"In any event, it sounds like Wolfreich was part of a military expedition that went to *their* Mars as part of an attempted 'conquest of space' that went really, *really* sideways. The people he found there tricked him into coming here–and apparently look enough like the Fortuned that he thought that Aelia, Astarte, and I were what he likes to call 'half-breeds'. In Aelia's case... he's not wrong.

"In my universe, there's a Fortuned colony on the far side of the Moon–territory they took from the Greys. I'm willing to bet there's one in Wolfreich's universe as well."

"Why so?"

"I hope this isn't a sensitive topic," I said, "but the gear plugged into Wolfreich's 'moon wog' looks an awful lot like the gear that was plugged into the original you the last time I saw him. I've never heard of the

Fortuned breaking up Selenite hives and turning them into slaves… but it's a big multiverse. I don't know *everything*."

"So, what happens next?" Case asked.

"Since Wolfreich couldn't beat or mindfuck what he wanted out of me, he's decided to make me an honorary white dude."

"Which, of course, is just another way to get what he wants. You've played this game before."

"More times than I like to think. You and I both know that this is going to *really* get ugly if he doesn't get what he's looking for."

"Which is what? A portal back to his own universe? Hell, you can't even get *yourself* home without the contents of a certain knapsack that seems to have conveniently gone missing."

"And of which the less said the better," I replied. "The portal back to his universe is right where he left it, in one of Mars' moons. But there's something else he needs to get there. I've managed to convince him I don't have it, but that's mostly because he keeps asking the wrong questions."

"Apparently he's not the only one," Case growled. "What does the son of a bitch want?"

"That's where it gets interesting."

* * *

"Oh, they don't call *themselves* 'Barsoomians.' I can't even pronounce what *they* say. A very fine gentleman of letters to whom I am distantly related invented the word 'Barsoom.' I borrowed it."

"Among other things," I said.

“Well, yes.” Wolfeich had sent for more wine, as well as food. At the far end of his tent, the captive Grey regarded me with unblinking black eyes and senses other than sight. I had no sense of it being in my mind, but I was sure that it was there for a reason.

“We had gone in search of an empire,” Wolfeich said as he topped off our glasses. “First to the Moon, then to Mars. But we were *sorely* disappointed.”

“And then you wound up here?”

“The Barsoomians lied to us,” Wolfeich said, his eyes narrowing. “And while I give you credit for being part-human and more white than not, don’t think for a *moment* that I will suffer being lied to again.”

“I’ve told no lies, Colonel. Even when your men were beating me, I answered questions as best I could.”

“Oh, I believe you, sir. But you are also not telling me what I need to know, not providing me what I require. This soon needs to end.

“My wog assures me it’s *here*. You told my men you did not know what they were talking about. I suspect this is just one of those little misunderstandings that happen from time to time. Before going to space, most of my men had hardly been anywhere, whereas I pride myself as a traveled man of the world. There was this one time I asked for a cigarette in Burma–and you would simply not *believe* what I got offered instead.”

“Hopefully an interesting experience.”

“Oh, it *was*... it was. It taught me the importance of not assuming that words always mean the same thing, even in *one* universe. I never bothered to learn Barsoomian–hardly seemed any need when we could use wogs to talk, and half the time I got the *distinct* impression the Barsoomians were already reading my mind, anyway.

"But there was one word I made a point of learning, an important word. I'm going to ask you one last time, Mr. Murphy: where is the *amoon jutoosh*?"

* * *

"The what?" Case asked.

"He mispronounced it," I said. "*Amun j'tauta'sh* means 'Dawn Matter.' When his men were interrogating me, they kept asking me 'where's the Wellesium?' and I kept telling them I didn't know what the fuck they were talking about.

"Eventually, they got tired of working me over and decided to use an enslaved Grey to mindfuck it out of me–only that didn't work, either."

"Mostly because she wasn't really trying, you know that, right?"

"She tried hard enough," I said. "Did you know she talked to me?"

Case's simulation froze for a long moment before he replied. "They don't *talk*, they manipulate dreams. They don't *really* know how to communicate with creatures like us."

"You can call what I was in a dream if you want to," I said. "All I know is that, at the end, she stopped pretending to be someone named 'Helene Abenard,' stopped pretending to be human altogether. She's not exactly what Wolfeich thinks."

"So the 'Wellesium' Wolfeich is looking for is some sort of Dawn Matter?"

"Or at least close enough that these so-called 'Barsoomians' call it by the same word. The... package I was sent here to deliver apparently has properties similar to 'Wellesium'–no surprise. So, it would seem, do an assortment of artifacts warehoused in Dayton, Ohio."

"You're kidding," Case said. "Wright-Patterson AFB?"

"That's not exactly what they call it here, but it is *exactly* what you're thinking. Except for it happening in this world's version of Texas, the Roswell Event happened here as well, with minor variations. Wolfeich's 'space force' didn't find what they were looking for there, either–but they found something else."

"Which would be?"

"Allies, apparently."

* * *

"You even got to meet the President?" I asked.

The dinner had been fairly decent, followed by cigars and brandy. If Wolfeich was planning to roll back into 'bad cop' mode, he was taking his sweet time with it–which was fine by me.

"Indeed I did, sir, and I could scarce believe my eyes. He's famous in my world as well–as an *entertainer*, not a politician. A cheap vaudevillian with criminal connections, one step ahead of bein' deported to a Freedom Zone."

I *had* to ask. "What's a 'Freedom Zone?'"

"In my 'United States,' there are 'Freedom Zones' and 'Opportunity Zones.' People livin' in Freedom Zones get to earn their freedom; people livin' in Opportunity Zones get to pursue opportunity."

“I’m just guessing here, but is it safe to say that the folks in ‘Freedom Zones’ are mostly brown and the folks in ‘Opportunity Zones’ are mostly white?”

“I suppose,” Wolfreich said, with a dismissive wave of his cigar. “I had already come to accept the idea of a ‘multiverse’–*had to* once I met the man I can only describe as my brother from another mother–but I hadn’t realized the scope of such a thing until that moment. If a man like John Donald Drumpfmann can be president, *anything* can be possible.”

I shuddered. “Yeah, no kidding.”

“At least in *my* universe, the man knew his proper place. *This* ‘John Drumpfmann’ has delusions of grandeur. He wants to ‘make America great again,’ apparently has no idea what a squalid little country *his* ‘America’ really is–really no room in it for ‘Freedom’ or ‘Opportunity’.”

“But, of course, you didn’t tell *him* that.”

“I didn’t see much point in telling him *anything,* outside of what he wanted to hear.”

“Obviously,” I said, helping myself to more brandy. “Does ‘John Drumpfmann’ have any idea how he winds up if you roll in with an occupation army?”

“Obviously *not,*” Wolfreich said, topping off his own glass. “But I’m prepared to humor the man until I get what I want... sort of the way I’m humoring *you*, Mr. Murphy.

“You advised me to ‘ask nicely’, and so I am. But the clock is running, No one on this world seems to know what ‘Wellesium’ or *amoon jutoosh* or whatever you prefer to call it even is–dear lord, they float airships with *hydrogen*–but you are no more from this world than I am.

“Either my wog is mistaken or you are lying. Either there is a hidden store of Wellesium somewhere in this temple or there is not. If not, I am neither going home, nor helping John Drumpfmann pursue revenge fantasies, or doing much of anything else. I’ll be *dying* here… and it makes no difference to me if I take a few people with me.

“You have three days to think it over, Mr. Murphy. Your sister wives will be the first, but they will *not* be the last. You are free to move about this compound as you like, while you think it over, but *don’t* try to leave–and don’t assume for a moment that I do *not* mean *exactly* what I say.”

* * *

“I’m surprised it took him so long,” Case said. “Terrorists usually start threatening hostages from the get-go.”

“Whatever the hell he is, he’s not a terrorist. He calls himself a ‘gentleman’–where he’s from, that might even mean something.”

“Yeah, maybe,” Case said. “It means exactly shit in this scenario. What are you going to do?”

“I think he may be in for a surprise if he thinks he can execute Astarte with a borrowed raygun, and the last time anyone threatened Aelia’s life, it provoked Astarte into… fairly extreme measures.”

“That’s not going to happen this time.”

“No, but the consequences for Wolfeich and his men could be just as fatal.”

“I’m guessing that just peeling out of here and letting shit sort itself out isn’t an option?”

"No," I said. "It isn't. If I had done what I was supposed to do when I got here, none of this would be happening. I have an obligation to fix the consequences."

"You don't know that, old buddy. If you'd delivered the goods instead of hiding them, it's just as likely this asshole would have them now."

"Yeah... maybe."

* * *

Finding out that angels were real had been less of a stretch for me than it might've been, for a lot of people. I'd learned folk magic at my *abuela's* knee, more ceremonial stuff from the inhuman bastards I work for. Years of working for those bastards had taught me that hardly *anything* is ever what it seems.

Which is probably why finding out that the slick-looking guy sitting at the end stool in one of the bars I'd adopted after my divorce was none other than Lucifer himself hadn't been *that* big a deal. It was *not* a great time in my life–I was equally prepared to believe in anything... or nothing at all. Helping Lucifer Morningstar end his exile and loneliness had helped me cope with my own losses. I still miss him, even if he was a high-handed son of a bitch.

Decades later, after I'd thought I'd retired from all this shit, I found out that the whole 'fallen angel' thing had played out as well on a recently discovered parallel Earth–and that, one way or another, the inhuman bastards I work for wanted to see *that* angel go home to God as well.

Except in the literal sense of the word, 'angels' are not anything my old Sunday School teacher would've recognized. They are cosmically powerful sentient concentrations of exotic matter from the beginning of time–*Amun j'tauta'sh...* 'dawn matter'.

The devices I'd been given to dispatch an angel from this world were not made of *Amun j'tauta'sh,* but something with similar properties that also happened to be highly unstable, once removed from a special containment vessel concealed in the bottom of what looked like an old knapsack.

Jewel-like pieces of alien hyper-technology, they were the size of small hand grenades that would have the explosive yield of a small nuke if improperly handled... or at least, so I had been told.

One was a deep emerald green, and would serve the same purpose as the shard of creation that had once granted Morningstar his wings. One was ruby red, and would cause a sufficient amount of inanimate Dawn Matter–leftover bits of creation or an angel too far gone to be restored–to collapse into a quantum black hole. The last one was sapphire blue, and would send a signal through an artificial wormhole that I wanted to be retrieved.

Or at least... so I had been told.

Ghost Case had expressed serious skepticism that I had been told the truth. He had a good point. I'd been told that the main reason Case Prime had been mutated into a 'Dawn Matter detector' was because The Fortuned had come to the conclusion that Dawn Matter–in *any* form–was simply too dangerous to risk letting it fall into the wrong hands–specifically, into the hands of their ancient enemies... the grey aliens they occasionally call 'Selenites.'

If this was true, then what made the most pragmatic sense was to ensure that *all three* of the devices I'd been given did the same thing–the option 'B' that involved causing any nearby Dawn Matter to collapse into its own black hole. Case had pointed out that lying to a local field asset was *exactly* the sort of thing *we* would've done, back in the old days when we both worked for The Company.

He'd also pointed out that being told I had been promoted to an elite inner circle of the people I work for was precisely the sort of bullshit we might've told some hapless local asset back in the day to ensure their loyalty.

In both instances... His logic was pretty close to irrefutable.

On the other hand, Evangeia's people–first The Order, then The Obligate–had invested a fair amount in me over the decades. In a game with stakes as high as entire planets, I knew better than to think of myself as anything other than a disposable asset... but not necessarily a *cheap* asset. They might actually see a value in getting me back.

All I could really do was keep an open mind... and hedge my bets where I could.

What Wolfreich's enslaved Grey could detect across continental distances, the mutated half-Grey remains of Case Prime had detected across universes. Because of a residual psychic awareness from the time he'd done unto me as Wolfreich's Grey had just done, Case Prime was aware of my location as well. Because my employers had opened a molecule-sized artificial wormhole between our worlds, Case Prime could send a one-way data feed that my implants could use to paint my target location onto a 'heads up' display on my optic nerve.

Only I didn't really need it.

Past a certain point... I had *known* where I was going. I just didn't know exactly what I'd find when I got there–although, given the location, I had a pretty good idea.

This world's version of the fallen angel I used to drink beer with had adopted a significantly different look and attitude, calling herself 'Astarte.' Unlike Morningstar, who had largely looked upon humankind as a form of entertainment, Astarte had taken a more active interest.

She had cast out alien intruders that I'd worked both for and against in my own world. She'd shielded, as best she could, humankind from their own worst impulses. Whereas Morningstar had only loved God and himself (more or less in that order), Astarte had extended her own love, millennia before, to include a half human/half Fortuned woman named Aelia.

I could appreciate that. I'd been more than a little friendly with Aelia's double in my own world–even though the differences between the two were almost as striking as the similarities. Aelia had organized *La Comuna de las Hermanas* in opposition to imperialism at roughly the same time her double, Evangeia de Lourdes, had been initiating the likes of John Dee and Francis Walsingham into a shadowy Order that *controlled* empires.

Centuries later, I'd been initiated into that same Order when Evangeia had needed a double agent in The Company. It had worked out well... until it didn't. Decades after that, a higher-order initiation had moved me up from the farm team and into Evangeia's own organization... and led to my current mission.

Given that history, my own sense of skepticism was barely less than Case's, even if I was occasionally inclined to give some small benefit of doubt.

Even so, I'd had doubts about my mission almost from the start, and so I had begun to set up a 'Plan B' almost as soon as I had arrived on this world. Once I realized that my mission would take me to a place I knew *very* well, those plans solidified rapidly.

Part of the reason I had kept the 'social interface' that gave Case access to my senses switched off during my final on-foot approach to this place was so I could complete my 'Plan B' arrangement without his knowledge. While it wasn't likely Case could be compromised, neither was it impossible. He couldn't spill what he didn't know.

And even if the location of 'the goods' got out… I'd taken other precautions as well. I'd tell Case what I could. As for the rest, he understood 'need to know' as well as I did.

* * *

"Clever," Case said. "I might've done exactly the same thing in your place."

I'd been inserted into this world wearing clothes that would blend in, carrying a backpack that had been fabricated to appear equally unnoteworthy. The pack had contained what looked like a locally manufactured service revolver, as well as a device that was basically a 3D printer, and–carefully concealed in a hidden bottom compartment–the containment apparatus holding the devices I'd been charged with delivering. Along the way, I'd picked up an old motorcycle that had been my transportation for most of the way.

But even before I'd left Oregon… I'd found a good use for the '3D printer.'

"I probably could've picked one up at a sporting goods store, but fabricating it was easy enough. Once I had a duplicate backpack, I could stash the *real* backpack along with my motorcycle, walk in here with the decoy. The bike was low on fuel, anyway."

"And because 'Social' was switched off at the time, I have no idea where this 'stash' location might be. I'm a little offended... but I get it. The fact that you *knew* you'd find a secure location raises an interesting question–but so does the fact that you basically gave up on the location data Real Me was sending about halfway through Mexico."

I had picked my words carefully. Even though my end of the conversation was a subvocal mutter, I could barely hear myself, shotgun mics and audio enhancement software were common enough on my own world. I couldn't rule out Wolfeich and his command having comparable tech of their own.

"You can speculate on that all you want," I said. "You *know* I'm not going to comment."

"Yeah, you've made that pretty clear. I don't currently have a 'need to know.' But one of these days... I'd *like* to know."

"Assuming we're both intact and conscious at the end of all this, you got it. Meanwhile, there's one last thing I want to discuss before I find out if I can get down from this tree without busting my ass."

"What would that be?" Case asked.

"Wolfreich's Grey. I've been thinking about the conversation I had with her after she gave up on interrogating me. I have the distinct impression she *also* knows more than she's sharing."

"Don't call her a 'Grey'," Case said, an odd expression on his face. "That's almost as bad as Wolfeich calling her a 'wog'."

"What do you want me to call her, then–'Helene'?"

"That's just a name she borrowed from someone else," Case said. "Call her 'Celeste'."

"Celeste?"

The odd expression became grim. "It was my mother's name."

"That's somewhat messed-up," I said. "But if it works for you, it works for me. *Celeste* knows way too much. She knows that I stashed the goods. And she knows about you–the *real* you. She said he's figured out a way to escape. Is that even possible?"

Case laughed in a particularly nasty way. "What–that she knows about 'Real Me', or that he could escape from the fucked-up shit your space-elf girlfriend did to him? There's a *lot* you don't know, old buddy... but you're about to find out."

# Part 2: Ellsberg Variations

## *one: kayce*

"How is it that *Hiram* gets to come home... and you do not?"

"Hiram is an admiral and has other responsibilities. I'm just a captain–and the other admirals seem to think this is a good idea."

Esmerelda sulked at me through the televisor. I couldn't tell if she was more annoyed by having to take my call at RCN headquarters, the fact that I wasn't home, or that Hiram Díaz had–in her view–apparently gotten away with something yet again.

The fact that I had gotten a promotion in the bargain impressed her not at all. 'It is overdue,' had been her sole response.

It felt like far more than a week since I'd last spoken to my wife–it felt like another lifetime, another universe. For a while, I had thought that might be *literally* true, when strange things started happening around Saul Ellsberg. But Saul had been right: once I saw her, I knew that my wife was still my wife.

I just wasn't totally sure I was still *me*.

I had been planning to resign from BSI and go back to teaching history at the Naval Academy. I was tired of having secrets from my wife, tired of Admiral Díaz's intrigues and machinations, tired of living in a world that made my pop's books look like a newspaper. I wanted to go back to living in the same world everyone else lived in.

"It's a temporary assignment," I said. "I need to manage a team of civilian contractors who are evaluating information the Texicans have offered to share with California. Once that evaluation is completed, I will be coming home as well."

"What about these Yanqui claims that you are some sort of spy that abducted one of their people? I expect no better of Hiram Díaz," she sniffed. "What has he gotten you into?"

I sighed. "Yanquis say all sorts of things. I can tell you that *nothing* you are hearing from the Estados concerning me is true. For now, my love, please just trust me–I plan to be done with this–done with *all* of it–and home as soon as I can be."

"Are these 'civilian contractors' *Tejanos*, corazon? Or is this something else you cannot talk about?"

"I am working with Texicans," I told her. "Past that, I can't really talk right now."

She sniffed again. "They are as vulgar and ignorant as Yanquis. If you must manage them, watch them *closely*."

"In some cases," I said, "you might be surprised."

* * *

"Based on reports from myself and Admiral Díaz," I said, "the admiralty's recommendation is that we proceed with the information sharing agreement proposed by General Bush.

"The admiralty intends to formalize this agreement under conditions of the Pacific Federation Treaty of 1929, which recognizes Texas as a non-aggressor North American State.

"While this formal agreement is finalized, I am to remain on assignment in Texas as an advisor, supervising Dr. Albion, Dr. Abenard, and Sr.

Ellsberg. Our job is to process the information being shared by the Republic of Texas, ensure reciprocal access to records from the project formerly referred to as 'Majestic,' and assist in the investigation of any other such information our joint task force may uncover.

"Admiral Díaz is to return to California with the *Morrison* by way of *Estados Unidos Mexicanos,* which is also a Treaty of '29 non-aggressor. I have been instructed to formally request an armed escort for *Morrison* under Article 3 of the Treaty. I don't need an *immediate* answer, General Bush... but the admiralty needs to know if this is acceptable."

"I need to clear it with President Richards," Bush replied. "But I reckon it's not gonna be a problem. Congratulations on the promotion, *Captain* Cullen."

"Thank you, sir." A promotion that came at the cost of being on assignment in Texas was one I could've done without. On the other hand, it's one I might've not seen anytime soon... under other circumstances.

I'd completed a secured conference call with members of the California Navy's Admiralty Council, who had asked some *very* pointed questions about everything that had happened to me since leaving San Francisco the week before.

And I had told them *everything*... including the parts I wasn't sure I believed.

When I'd first arrested Saul Ellberg on espionage charges, he was just a middle-aged Sci-Rom writer who was being fed classified information that he'd been foolish enough to publish. But since most of that information was being fed to him via *dreams*... it wasn't really all that foolish... just extremely inconvenient.

That arrest, a year ago, had been largely for the purpose of getting Saul under contract to BSI. As a contractor, we could put him under fairly deep psychiatric analysis to find out more about these 'dreams'–as well as pay him to help analyze a growing body of evidence that the things in his dreams were literally *invading* our world.

Along the way, Saul began to demonstrate what can only be called 'psychic powers'–in response to which Admiral Díaz had decided to take Saul along for the annual 'Majestic' conference in *los Estados Unidos*. He had thought that Saul's abilities might reveal what the Yanquis members of the Majestic project were hiding–and why, after 50 years of cooperation, they were now lying to us.

Well... now we knew.

"My congratulations as well, Captain," Admiral Díaz said. "In my own view, your work over the last year has very much justified a promotion.

"I will confirm your orders and mine after this meeting. As soon as we can confirm the details of the requested escort, I will make preparations for *Morrison's* departure.

"But for now, given that this will be the *only* joint task force meeting I can attend in person, I wish to hear from the rest of General Bush's team."

Bush nodded. I'd had varying opinions about George Washington Bush over the days since I'd met him. A thoroughly unserious man, I could not imagine him achieving rank or authority anywhere but Texas. But if it wasn't for him, my entire team would probably be Yanquis hostages–if not in one of their damned camps, most likely under guard by their new allies.

"Agreed," Bush said. "Lindsay, you go first."

Seated next to General Bush was a tall, gray-haired woman wearing dungarees, a corduroy jacket, and a dark shirt with a muted plaid pattern. She'd been introduced to us as 'Senior Agent Lindsay Lochardt, Texas Department of Public Safety Special Operations Division'–basically a Texican working for a civilian Texas version of BSI.

"Got it, G.W." She stood. "Captain Cullen and team," she said, "welcome to Texas. I'm here to share information my team has developed from intelligence received from the asset code-named 'Ghost One'."

I wasn't sure why they felt the need to use a code name in a confidential briefing, but I also had no idea how much the Texicans did–or did not–compartmentalize their intelligence.

Or maybe it was just convenient shorthand for a complicated reality. 'Ghost One' referred to both a 'ghost airship' that had crashed in Texas a hundred years before, and that ship's pilot–a partly mechanical nonhuman calling himself 'Ruhl Skattersmythe', who had spent most of that hundred years in an unmarked grave in Aurora, Texas.

My team had engaged in a certain amount of code-naming as well, with names like 'Project Ikelos,' 'Project Oneiros,' and 'Project Phantasos' for the work we were doing. Strip away Admiral Díaz's fondness for the classical and the dramatic... and it was largely the same thing.

And anyone who'd actually *met* Ruhl would understand *immediately,* referring to both pilot and ship as 'ghosts.'

Agent Lochardt stood and walked to a map of North America on the far wall of the conference room. A number of hand-drawn crossmarks picked out locations on the map with what looked like timestamps and other notations. Three lines connected a number of the crossmarks... but not all of them.

“Let’s start with a little back-story,” she said, picking up a map pointer. “DPS Special Ops doesn’t have a lot of history with this sort of thing. We mostly do counter-terrorism, deep-cover asset management, and investigating security threats. No one who works for BSI is gonna be surprised that we have working assets in the U.S., California, Canada, the unincorporated territories, and Mexico. We also have access to the North American Air Safety Information System... although, these days, that’s mostly automated.

“In other words, we already *had* a network in place when General Bush asked us to start validating ‘Ghost One’ information–*only* that’s *not* what we were told we were validating: all my team received were locations, timestamps, and a very vague idea of what we were lookin’ for–basically, just look for reports of anything ‘unusual.’

“That was three years ago. I eventually got ‘Ghost One’ clearance; my team hasn’t, but it’s a pretty safe bet they’ve figured this is *not* standard ‘intelligence.’ A year later, I also set up a second team, walled off from the first, and gave them *very* specific instructions: find and catalogue ‘unidentified aerial phenomena’ reports–again, starting from roughly three years ago.

“We wanted to accomplish two things with the second team. First: double-check ‘Ghost One’–find out if conventional systems were picking up UAPs that Ghost One *wasn’t* reporting. Second: confirm the accuracy of the data. At this point, I’m about ready to find the second team another assignment: the data from Ghost One is consistently reliable and high-quality. The UAP reports that *don’t* turn up in Ghost One’s reporting are pretty much all ‘false positives’–swamp gas and the like.

“Any questions so far, Admiral Díaz?”

The admiral shook his head. “Please continue.”

“About a year ago,” Agent Lochardt said, “both the frequency and the characteristics of the ‘Ghost One’ reports began to change–more reports, and the reports started getting... well, *strange*. In the last month, things have gotten even stranger–and that’s where this map comes in.

“This first track,” she ran the map pointer from a starting point at the map’s upper left corner along a line drawn to a point near the map’s center, then down another line to a point near the map’s bottom, “points out a series of anomalous ground targets Ghost One picked up at various points in Oregon, Texas, and Central America, after an object tracked in from deep space briefly touched down off the Oregon Coast last month.

“The second track,” she moved the pointer to a crossmark near the top of the map, “follows the path of an object we’re calling ‘Ghost Two’ from an initial atmospheric entry above the Arctic Circle to an apparent intercept,” she followed the line down into Texas, “with one of the ground targets. After that,” she followed a line to the right with the pointer, “the object veered East into the U.S., where it remained stationary until two days ago–at which time,” she followed a line to the same point at the bottom of the map, “it apparently converged with the last ground target in Central America.

“Last, but not least, *this* last track,” she ran the pointer from West to East, starting at a point close to San Francisco, “follows a set of airborne anomalies that appeared last week at various points over the Sierra Madres, the Wasatch Range, and the Appalachians. It also lines up with roughly 80% of the standard airship flight path from San Francisco to Dayton, Ohio–where ‘Ghost Two’ happened to be for the better part of a week.”

"The week *we* were there," I said. "Right?"

"Correct, Captain Cullen."

### *two: murphy*

"I had expected we would be having this conversation," Sister Guadalupe Concepcion Hernandez said. "You know they listen to us, yes?"

"Of course," I said. "But what's the likelihood of them understanding?" We were speaking in a local Mayan dialect that I could never have understood without my implants, seated on stone benches to one side of the open space where *La Comuna de las Hermanas* conducted group exercises and meditations every day at sundown.

Currently, those exercises were being conducted under the watch of 'The Barsoom Expeditionary Force'–men in black tactical gear and body armor that looked a lot like stuff I'd have worn once, only armed with what I was thinking of as 'phaser rifles.' The guns also reminded me of stuff I've seen before, but these guys should *not* be packing this shit–their commander had all but confirmed it was stolen.

A few feet away, the ghost of Colvin Case pretended to lounge against a tree, pretending to be dressed in the same leather and dungarees I'd worn halfway across a continent before winding up here. I wasn't planning on telling Sister Guadalupe anything I wasn't cool with him hearing, and he might just have a useful opinion on whatever she was willing to say.

"They have a way of listening," Sister Guadalupe replied. "That will not be bothered by any language–as you well know."

"I know what they have," I told her. "I made a deal with it. That's not a problem for now."

“Then you are indeed resourceful, oh man of another world.” Skin the color of old tobacco with a smile to match and gray-streaked dark hair, she had made plain her disapproval of me from the moment we’d met. I couldn’t tell if she was currently being respectful or sarcastic... it probably would’ve come off the same, either way.

“Just call me Murphy,” I said. “Everyone knows I ain’t from around here.”

“So it would seem, Murphy. Now, what is it you wish to know of me?”

I had met her two weeks earlier when I had been killing time on the Mexican border while I waited for the riverboat that took me close enough to my destination that an old motorcycle could get me most of the rest of the way on a trip I eventually had to finish on foot. The forgotten temple I’d been led to was outlined against the setting sun behind us.

And when I’d arrived here... Sister Guadalupe had been here to greet me.

The explanation could be something as mundane as an elderly *herborista* having a private helicopter, but was far more likely to involve the various forms of magic that were both more common and more potent in this Earth than mine.

I didn’t particularly care one way or the other, but I did want to know just how much her and the other members of *La Comuna* were *really* at risk from Colonel Wolfreich and his hearty band of Space Pirates. They’d given me two days to give up the goods they thought I was sitting on, at which time they intended to start taking out hostages. I didn’t think it was going to be that simple... but I had to *know*.

“I’m not going to ask how you got here,” I told her. “Not my business, really. But I want to know if you or another of the others are able to escape the same way. I also need to know if the same trick can get Astarte or Aelia away from here as well, before the shooting starts.”

“The Elder Sisters do not leave their home. Astarte is bound here in ways I do not understand. Aelia is bound to Astarte in ways anyone who has ever loved understands all too well.

“As for the others? The senior sisters of The Commune may travel as I did, but we will not leave our younger sisters and husbands to the mercy of idiot gringos with guns–no offense.”

“None taken,” I told her. “I’m only half gringo, and I agree that they *are* idiots–but, as you say, they are idiots with guns.”

She snorted. “Like all gringos, they confuse their guns with their manhood–and in this case, *both* are borrowed property. They are much mistaken if they think we are helpless hostages.

“But even so, there is much harm they could do–would you want to see a *child* done unto as they did your cell door or the commune gate?”

The way she said it gave me a sudden thought. “How many have they killed so far?”

“There are injuries, but none dead. Aelia bade us to not resist.”

“How many are they?” I asked.

“Difficult to tell one from another under their helmets, but I have never seen more than a dozen or so at once... that may be all there is.”

“Interesting...” I said.

The thought I was forming was either going to be a little too late or a little too soon.

“They confiscated the Moon Knives on arrival,” I said. “Does the Commune have other weapons?”

Sister Guadalupe smiled a smile that would have been nasty even with perfect dental hygiene. “What they were *permitted* to take can be recalled at any time. We require no *other* weapons to defend ourselves.”

“You mean... under ordinary circumstances.”

“Well, yes,” she admitted.

“Assuming these gringos no longer had the use of their fancy guns,” I said, “what else would the Commune require to defend themselves?”

“We would require only Aelia’s permission to act.”

“I’ll see what I can do about it.”

“Is it permitted to ask why you are here?” she suddenly asked. “Or is that a secret between you and The Sisters?”

*That* was a good question. As an Obligate field agent, I had fairly broad discretion to act, so no problem with my ‘orders.’ The only thing Astarte had asked of me so far was to ‘try not to die.’ Aelia had asked nothing at all.

“I’m here to help,” I told her. “Do you know what The Sisters *truly* are?”

“The Chronicles of the Commune tell us that Aelia’s kind once ruled the world,” Sister Guadalupe said. “Once openly, then in secret–until Astarte banished them. Are you of Aelia’s kind? You look it.”

“In a way,” I said. “What do you know of Astarte?”

“The Chronicles say that she has sat at Aelia’s side for over a thousand years–changeless, except for what it cost her to close this world. I know that it is by her power that this valley is as closed to the world as the world itself is closed–or once was. I know that she is immortal. But among us... only Aelia knows Astarte’s true nature.”

"I know it as well," I told her. "I was sent by–let's just say I was sent by 'Aelia's kind.' I was sent to assist the immortal Astarte in leaving this world."

"You mean you were sent as an assassin?"

"Well, that's *one way* of leaving the world," I replied. "And Aelia's people provided that option... but that's not really what they claim to have in mind–and it's not really what I have in mind, either."

"You would not be in this place did Astarte and Aelia not permit it," Sister Guadalupe said. "I am willing to accept the idea that you are 'here to help'."

"Aren't you going to ask me about Astarte's 'true nature'?"

She shook her head. "Even *Aelia* describes her people as liars. I would not assume you had been told the truth, even if I were inclined to believe *you*. Do you have a plan for dealing with these idiot gringos?"

"I have what might be called a 'concept of a plan'."

She snorted. "Is it as worthless as it sounds?"

"Well... I'm working on it."

"Then you'd better work *fast*," said the voice of Ghost Case. "Company coming."

A shadow fell over me in the fading light as one of Wolfreich's men loomed over me. "You and this old bitch are breakin' curfew, *boy*," came a familiar voice–it was the same guy who'd taken me prisoner in the first place.

“Mummy and Daddy are talking,” I told him, switching to a language and a tone he’d understand. “Colonel Wolfreich gave orders to leave me the fuck alone–what, you didn’t get the memo?”

“Guess I filed it where I’m about to file *you*,” he said, as he raised the barrel of the gun.

### *three: ellsberg*

Admiral Díaz turned to General Bush. “You *knew*,” he said.

“Not *everything*,” Bush replied. “I was already booked to go to the airshow before this ‘Ghost Two’ stuff started happenin’. I had no choice except to go through with it. I figured you *might* show up–I did *not* expect what wound up happenin’.”

“*No one* did,” the Admiral said. “I went there to find out what the Yanquis have been lying about. I did *not* expect them to attempt to make me a hostage. If this ‘Ghost Two’ object was at Patterson Aerodrome at the same time as the conference... It raises disturbing questions.”

Just possibly, I thought, it also provides some answers.

“*Everything* that happened at Patterson raises questions,” Bush said. “And not just the stuff I ain’t supposed to know about. There was some funny stuff goin’ on at the airshow as well. Part of the reason I was able to help y’all get outta Dayton was ‘cause I’d already decided to peel out early myself.

“But that’s another thing we can talk about later. Right now, Hiram, I want to know what else you need from my team before you head back to Cali.”

I was trying to figure out why Helene & I weren't going back to California as well. I could understand keeping Ameryst here, understand keeping Kayce here to keep an eye on her. *Maybe* I was being kept here because I was on the extremely short list on non-Texicans who had ever met 'Ghost One.'

Or maybe not. If Kayce had told the admirals *everything*... maybe they wanted me in Texas for a reason. And maybe there was a reason I hadn't been interrogated *yet*.

I'd soon be finding out.

"I need to better understand how you are acquiring this tracking data from 'Ghost One'," Díaz said. "*Nothing* I saw at the facility we visited indicated any such level of system integration."

"That's probably a question for me," said the younger man sitting across from me. Thin and boyish, Charley Hardin had been introduced as an engineer on permanent load from Hughes Aeronautics. *All* of the technical innovations that had led to resurrecting 'Ghost One' were essentially his doing.

Bush nodded and Hardin proceeded. "We can't really see what Ruhl–sorry, 'Ghost One'–sees. We don't even understand how the sensors work. So, no: there is no 'system integration' as such.

"Instead, I rigged up a system based on a game console that lets Ghost One use a joystick to paint targets into a graphic representation of North American airspace from ground level out to... well, theoretically, to infinity. The edge of the solar system, for sure. The system captures coordinates, time of entry, and target classification into a database I've set up for secure remote access."

"Can you explain this classification schema?" Díaz asked.

"Uh, yeah," Hardin said. "It pretty much breaks down into what Ghost One considers 'friendlies' versus 'hostiles'–*his* criteria, not ours–versus 'anomalies'. The anomalies are *really* 'unidentified objects': stuff that Ghost One doesn't understand any better than we do. There seems to be a lot of that these days."

Díaz turned to General Bush. "Am I to understand, Jorge, that *all* of the tracking data you are offering to share was entered *manually* into your database... by 'Ghost One'?"

"Thanks, Charley," Bush said, then turned to the admiral. "Yep, that's right, Hiram. Manually entered by Ghost One, then double-vetted by two different teams of analysts–because I'm not any more inclined than you are to trust intel from 'unconventional sources' without finding a way to check it.

"You're welcome to triple-check against your own records. If you like–in fact, I would kinda encourage it."

"My fellow admirals will likely agree with you," Díaz said. "I am concerned as well about this 'ground target' business. What else can you tell me about that?"

"Not a lot," Agent Lochart said. "Like I said, we had a 'Ghost One' report on something tracked in from deep space that seems to have actually touched down in the vicinity of Astoria, Oregon.

"Not long after that, we also started getting 'Ghost One' reports of something tracking intermittently on the ground–*not* an aerial contact, and *not* something that can be tracked continuously. But I've been able to get field agents to the locations where 'Ghost Two' is supposed to have showed up as well. And my agents confirm what 'Ghost One' is reporting."

"Why do you call it 'Ghost Two'?" I asked.

Agent Lochart returned to her seat, handing me a few sheets of stapled paper. “Here’s one of the eyewitness accounts,” she said.

I scanned over it, handed it to Kayce, who scanned it even more quickly and handed it to Díaz. “Point taken,” he said. “What about this reported sighting in Central America?”

“We’re still working on it,” Agent Lochart said. “It’s in a pretty remote place.”

“*How* remote?” Díaz asked.

“*I* can field that one,” said the man seated between Lochardt and Hardin. As tall as Admiral Díaz and even broader, Major T.J. Kuehng was dressed in black fatigues, a gray flight jacket and a gray Texican-style vaquero hat. On the breast of the flight jacket: an embroidered patch showing a stylized map of the original Republic of Texas overlaid with the face of a laughing devil–the insignia of *Los Diablos Tejanos*... Texas Rangers Special Forces.

The admiral smiled. “I suspected you might, *Tomas*.”

“Been a minute and a half, ain’t it, Hiram?” The expression on Major Kuehng’s face wasn’t quite General Bush’s typical smirk... but it didn’t miss it by much. He turned to Kayce. “Your boss, me, and G.W. *all* spent some time in that neck o’ the woods back in the day, Captain Cullen... *too* much time, really.”

He turned back to the admiral. “That ‘location’ in Central America is pretty much just a patch of jungle in the Guatemalan Highlands. There is *somewhat* reliable riverboat service to within 50 klicks or so–but you’re pretty much on foot after that.

“So I recall,” Admiral Díaz said. “Or via air.”

“Unless y’all are plannin’ on making another ‘Article Three’ request, we can’t just send stuff into Central American airspace,” Kuehng replied. “At least not *conventional* stuff. My boys are workin’ on a way to get some decent intel–let’s talk about it later.”

Admiral Díaz nodded. “Many thanks, Major Kuehng. Agent Lochart, do you have anything else?”

“Not really, sir. We’ve developed a ‘person of interest’ profile, based on the two reported sightings we’ve been able to investigate, circulated it to any DPS field office that we think might be on the ‘ground target’s’ path. So far, nothing has turned up.”

“Please make me aware if anything does,” Díaz said. “Mr. Hardin, thank you for overviewing your data collection system. Is there anything else you would like to share at this time?”

“About ‘Ghost One’?” Hardin replied. “Not really. You’ve met him; you know what we’re dealing with.” He turned and looked at me. “But I know what ‘Ghost One’ told *you*, Mr. Ellsberg. If you’d like to find out more… I might just know a way.”

### four: murphy

Like I said… idiots.

Getting within dick-wagging distance was a mistake… but he probably didn’t know that.

I stood up fast–*very* fast–driving my right arm up, fingers curled but not forming a fist, elbowing the barrel of his weapon to one side. There was a flash of light in the corner of my eye, but I didn’t bother to see what it was. Reaching under his chin, I wrapped my fingers around his helmet’s chinstrap, pulling his head down hard into the rising fist of my left arm.

The visor shattered, his nose broke, and he went down hard. On the way down, I ripped the weapon from his grasp and threw it to the ground. I also ripped away his helmet, throwing it on top of the weapon.

From a sprawled, seated position, he glared up at me and produced what looked like a hunting knife from somewhere in his gear–Sister Guadalupe, now kneeling next to him, had also produced a stiletto from somewhere on her person–a stiletto firmly pointed against his carotid artery.

I kicked the helmet and the weapon further away from him. Helmet gone, I could see that he had buzzcut red hair and pale skin–or maybe the blood pumping from his nose made him seem more pale than he really was.

That's about when my reflexes slowed to the speed of an unmodified human being. That's when I also realized that the flash I'd been too busy to look at was the bench I'd been sitting on getting turned to dust like a cheap sci-fi special effect.

"As a matter of curiosity," I asked him, "did you even bother to read that 'memo' before you filed it? What *did* Wolfreich tell you?"

"He said to leave you alone as long as you didn't try to leave or start any trouble–what the fuck do you call *this*?"

"An error in judgment," I said, holding my hands where the soldiers now surrounding me could see them. "Yours, not mine."

I nodded to Sister Guadalupe, who made the stiletto disappear and stood next to me.

He gained his feet, retrieving his weapon–but leaving the helmet on the ground.

He put the barrel of the weapon under my chin and pushed up. I knew he wasn't going to pull the trigger. When he leaned in close enough to spit blood in my face, he confirmed it.

"The colonel gave you three days, boy–startin' *yesterday*. Three days before we start takin' out hostages–startin' with them other halfbreeds, but this old bitch just got moved up to *next*. Whatever the hell you *think* you're planning? *Forget about it*. As of now, you're confined to quarters.

"Maybe I can't touch you yet–but the only reason you're still here is because the Colonel wants something, and he thinks you're gonna give it to him. Once he stops thinkin' that, you're *mine*, boy.

"*All* mine."

* * *

I was returned to my cell after that, with a guard posted at my door. It didn't look like I was going anywhere until Colonel Wolfreich was ready for another little chat... but I was okay with that.

"Since you weren't looking in that direction," Case said, "I don't know if he'd already pulled the trigger or not. Is it really a theory you want to put to the test?"

"Unless we can figure out something else," I said. "We may not have any choice."

As a kid growing up watching *Star Trek*, I hadn't thought much about it.

But I did later.

You're on a starship–or, for that matter, in *any* kind of military setting. You have *hundreds* of people under your command, and every... single.. *one* of them has access to sidearms that can put a hole in a bulkhead or someone they think might be cheating at cards or cheating on *them,* or put a hole in anyone or anything else they might have a real or perceived grievance with–or maybe just vaporize whatever they're pissed off about.

The guy who invented *Star Trek* had some pretty optimistic ideas about what humanity was likely to be like by the time people in color-coordinated turtlenecks got to run around the galaxy with the equivalent of a tac nuke as a sidearm.

The aliens I know who already *have* those kind of sidearms... are not optimists.

"What makes you think they're bluffing, anyway?" Case asked. "Is there something *else* you're keeping to yourself?"

"No," I said. "It's a combination of common sense and experience with technology these guys haven't had. Everything Wolfreich's troops have either looks like it came from the 'Soldier of Fortune' mail-order catalog or the latest sci-fi space opera franchise–and *nothing* in between.

"The sci-fi looking stuff looks suspiciously familiar. I think they stole it from Aelia's people, who are either a close analog to Evangeia's people or *exactly* the same... and I know how *their* tech works.

"That 'fake service revolver' I was given for this mission doesn't have a 'vaporize' setting–but it defaults to 'nonlethal' and it is keyed to *me.* Anyone else who tries to use it for *anything*... is shit out of luck.

"I can't believe The Fortuned would *ever* produce weapons of this capability that didn't have similar restrictions. Say whatever else about them you want... they're not *stupid.*"

"You might be right," Case said. "But that guy whose nose you just busted was also packing a Bowie knife and what looked like a conventional pistol as a sidearm. Even if they just use clubs, they can still take out hostages... if they think that's what it takes to make you give up what they want."

"Sister Guadalupe thinks there might not be more than a dozen of these guys, and I think she might be right. That 'ghost airship' they arrived in isn't exactly a troop carrier. She also thinks her and the other sisters might be able to take these guys, minus their guns–and she might be right about that as well."

"Even if those old ladies are total bad-asses, it could still get messy," Case said. "We need other options."

"Perhaps I can help," said another, familiar, voice.

Slowly, I turned my head. As expected, the mottled golden serpent was again coiled at the foot of my bed, the last foot or so of its body holding the head aloft as if to make a meal of some hapless rodent.

"I think introductions are in order," Astarte continued. "I know that you are not merely talking to *yourself.*"

## *five: ellsberg*

I wasn't surprised to find that the guesthouse that was apparently going to be home for a while had a rooftop deck with a great view of the airship field, even less surprised to find that the deck was equipped with a full bar. Texas hospitality being what it is, the fact that there was a bar was no surprise at all.

As we watched and sipped our drinks, the blunt arrowhead shape of the *Morrison* cast off and rose, slowly pivoting to face south. When it reached cruising altitude, the autogyro escort wing fell into formation around it. Then the turbo impellers on the *Morrison's* stubby wings lit, and the entire formation moved over the low hills and quickly out of sight.

“Anyone else feeling a little... abandoned?” I asked.

“Not really,” Kayce said, after a sip of scotch. “I’m sure none of you are particularly happy to still be in Texas, but I promise to do everything I can to make this a short stay.”

“I shall certainly miss Hiram,” Helene said. “But I do not envy what awaits his return.”

“I think he’ll be fine,” Kayce said. “Admiral Díaz has taken heavier fire than getting grilled by other admirals–and at least he got to go home.”

Overstuffed chairs surrounded a gas-fired firepit that hadn’t seemed necessary until the sun went down. Ameryst Albion sat in the chair furthest from the bar. Catching my glimpse, she smiled. “I like Admiral Díaz,” she said, “but I barely know him. It’s not the same for me as it is for the rest of you.”

“There’s a few things I need you all to understand,” Kayce said, as she walked over to the bar to refresh her drink.

“First, I need you to know that this building is now being routinely swept by a countermeasures team attached to the California Embassy. You still need to watch what you say under other circumstances... but not here.

“Next: even though you are civilian contractors, every one of your contracts includes a ‘state of emergency’ addendum. You are hereby under notice that we are, indeed, operating under ‘state of emergency’ conditions.

“Lastly,” she said. “On the off chance that you do not all equally understand the implications of an ‘Article Three’ request from the California Navy, I need to make that clear as well.”

“Is this another of your ‘history lessons’?” I asked.

“Only a short one,” she replied. “The Treaty of 1929 doesn’t just confirm the Pacific Federation as a mutual defense organization. It also makes very clear the relationships between member states, recognized non-aggressor states… and the aggressor states that made the treaty necessary in the first place.

“The very moment the *Morrison* crosses into Mexican airspace with a requested military escort from Texas… the provisions of Article Three go into effect.”

“And this is important,” I said. “Why?”

“It’s important,” she replied, “because it supersedes *any* mutual defense agreements between Texas and *Los Estados*. If the Yanquis and their Russian allies hadn’t backed down from their attempted land grabs… there could’ve been a world war.

“When *Los Estados* tried to grab the Nicaragua Canal back in the Nineties, *República Federal de Centro América* made an ‘Article Three’ request as well. Texas responded, the Yanquis backed down… again.

“The moment *Morrison* crosses from Texican airspace into Mexico, Texas shifts from being a ‘non-aggressor’ and becomes a Federation *ally* state… which means the Yanqui *Presidente* can bleat all he wants. The Texicans aren’t handing us over–or doing anything else that might be seen as aiding a Treaty of ‘29 aggressor state.”

“Are you truly sure of that?” Helene asked. “The Yanqui *Presidente* seems to enjoy support among a great many Texicans.”

“No one in power,” Kayce replied. “President Richard’s party has been Pro-Pacific for *decades*. They aren’t going to squander that.

"I *will* get us all to California–including you, Dr. Albion, if that's still what you want–as soon as I can. You're my responsibility now. But please understand: there may be things beyond my control."

"*Completely* understood, Captain Cullen," Ameryst said. "Please don't worry about me at *all*–I'm finally getting to do what I've wanted to do my entire life!"

Kayce smiled. "Outside of business hours, you can just call me 'Kayce.' I admire your resilience, Dr. Albion, even if I'm not sure I share it."

"If you're 'just Kayce,' I'm 'just Ameryst'–but thanks."

Kayce turned to me. "How about you, Saul? Other than feeling a 'little abandoned,' are you okay?"

"Ask me again this time tomorrow," I said.

"You can still back out," she said. "I'll tell the Texicans the deal is off."

"No, I can do this–and I don't think you understand, Kayce. If what Hardin proposed works, I am just as much getting what I want as Ameryst is getting what she's always wanted."

Kayce turned to Helene. "Any last thoughts on this from you, Helene?"

Helene shook her head. "What the Texicans are suggesting amounts to enhanced interrogation that has been banned by almost every country on Earth. My objections to this are already on record–and they stand.

"On the other hand," she turned to Saul. "*You* have agreed to do this willingly. And perhaps you *will* finally have the answers you have always wanted.

* * *

"It's the same tank we used to resuscitate Ruhl–hope that's okay."

The cylinder in front of me more than a little resembled the one I'd seen at the Majestic Conference, just bigger. Only appropriate, given that Ruhl Skattersmythe is at least three times the size of the grey alien I'd seen floating in the cylinder there.

It still tore at me to think about it. The thing in the tube had screamed in my mind, screamed endlessly. To escape that scream, I had caused a thing to happen, or something had reached out through me to make that thing happen.

If this worked, maybe I would *finally* know.

"Ruhl was *dead*–you've cleaned it, right?"

Charley Hardin grinned lopsidedly at me. "He was only *mostly* dead. But, yeah–we scrubbed it out."

Charley was a skinny brown-skinned kid with curly, bleached-blond hair and bright eyes behind glasses with thick, dark rims. About half my age, he was insanely brilliant and apparently well-known within his field. Ameryst knew him by reputation and was deeply impressed that he'd managed to resurrect an actual 'aethernaut'–even though Ruhl Skattersymthe has mostly resurrected himself.

Nothing Charley had shared at the joint task force meeting had really surprised me. I already knew that the 'ghost airships' and 'mystery disks' had come from competing alien species. I already knew that one of these species–Ruhl's–was a lot more human than the other.

Unfortunately, the species that appeared to be talking to me via dreams and using me as some sort of drone was the *less* human variety–the thing

I'd seen at Patterson. No one was ever going to just *talk* to them, the way I had talked to Ruhl.

Even more unfortunate was that the aliens feeding information into my dreams had pretty much *stopped* talking, yielding the floor to someone else. Someone who presented as human... and claimed to have been even more massively interfered with by aliens than *I'd* been.

The information 'Colvin Case' was sharing with me was potentially valuable, but it was even more fantastic than the idea of an 'aethernaut' scooting around the Texas badlands on a motorcycle. I needed to find a way to validate it.

And the only way I could do that was by going back to the source. And Charley Hardin thought he knew a way to make that happen.

A technician took my glasses while another began to zip the hood over my face.

"After this," Charley said, "You aren't going to *hear* anything, *see* anything, or *feel* anything–not until we peel you out. You can still decline to do this... last chance."

"I'm good," I said. "Let's do this."

The hood went into place, and he was right.

There was nothing.

* * *

Floating in that void, I quickly realized why this was considered 'torture'. But I also realized why it might just work.

The Texicans had a revived alien, had alien tech that could track other aliens anywhere in the solar system. California had fifty years of notes on their share of a similar project that had produced... basically, nothing. Unless you count finding the power switch on a crashed flying saucer.

But they also had *me*.

Once Ruhl Skattersmythe confirmed that I was, indeed, 'infected with dreams,' it was only a matter of time before the effort to find the source of those dreams escalated. At least no one had suggested digging around in my brain for a *physical* source for the infection.

At least... not *yet*.

Also confirmed, at least in part, was the *Morrison's* interrupted journey to Dayton, Ohio, which I'd originally thought was somehow *my* doing. Ruhl had tracked the unknowns that had surrounded the *Morrison* before it moved–*not*, as I'd thought at the time, to another universe. The actual move was simply from one side of a mountain to another. Once *Morrison* was away from the alien tech that had caused their failure, its engines restarted and we continued on to Patterson Aerodrome... and everything that awaited there.

What I hadn't known, but wasn't surprised to find out, was that it had happened more than once–which went a long way toward explaining the messed-up memories everyone had of that trip.

Ruhl also confirmed that I had apparently–to use Ameryst's term–'teleported' my entire team out of a locked auditorium. But there was no other corroborating evidence. Even though the Yanquis' mad presidente had stopped short of declaring war on the rest of North America, getting in or out of the immediate vicinity of Patterson Aerodrome was still going to be difficult–even if Agent Lochardt's ground assets could find eye witnesses who *weren't* under custody.

The Texicans had offered California a *lot* by sharing the secret of Ruhl Skattersmythe, had a right to expect a lot in return–a lot more than just the archive data of a fifty year long project to uncover the secrets of another alien crash... a project that had basically failed.

And the only other asset California had to offer... was me.

The dreams that started it all have apparently gone away. There's just the one dream now, where I dream I'm talking to someone the aliens have fucked over far worse than they ever fucked over me. Knowing it could be worse doesn't make me love my situation any better.

I can't tell if I'm speaking aloud or not, remembering things or making things up. I can't tell if I'm really here or if I'm even real–even real to myself.

Charley seems to think this treatment is either going to trigger another conversation or traumatize me into 'teleporting' again. The possibility I could walk away from this with even worse mental problems than the ones I started out with... doesn't seem to have occurred to him.

Or maybe he doesn't care, or maybe he and the others are conspiring against me. I have no idea what he and Ameryst really talked about when they went to see Ruhl. Maybe he *really* likes Ameryst, noticed that she sort of has a crush on me, and figured out a way to get me out of the way.

Dear god–am I *really* thinking this shit?

Maybe I'm undoing everything the *one* therapist who didn't think I was crazy managed in a year–or maybe Helene's part of the conspiracy that put me in this fucking tube. I've wondered a few times if she was *really* human... maybe not.

Maybe *none* of them are–and maybe they have no intention of ever taking me out of this fucking tank. If I started screaming, would it even matter?

Would I even *know*?

### *six: murphy*

"I'm surprised you're surprised, to be honest. I figured this sort of thing would be well within your abilities. "

"Yes and no," the serpent said. "I knew there was a fairly detailed hologram of what appears to be a somewhat human brain stored in your implants. But I had no idea why–much less that it would be self-aware or sentient."

"Well, 'it' is," Case said. "And I'm right the fuck here. *Happy* to answer any questions you might have about my self-awareness or sentience."

"Is it always this insolent?" the serpent asked.

"Pretty much," I said. "But as long as it's useful, I pretty much don't care–and much of what Case has done recently has been *very* useful."

"I accept your judgment in this, Murphy."

I knew that the voice in my head was being created by what *looked* like a particularly colorful tree boa poised on the foot of my bed, that I had first seen draped across the shoulders of the being *La Comuna de las Hermanas* venerated as 'Astarte.' But I also knew that both the inhumanly beautiful Astarte and her pretty pet snake were just disguises–'puppets,' Morningstar had called them–a relatable form taken on by an incomprehensible and utterly inhuman thing from the dawn of time.

Sometimes also referred to as an 'angel.'

"I had thought you might return," I said, "now that I am no longer being interrogated. I assume you know I am operating under something of a deadline."

I was speaking in the same local dialect I'd used when I met with Sister Guadalupe, but at the same low mutter I always used when I was talking to Case. Neither Case nor Astarte were telepaths, but both had senses unavailable to anyone who might be eavesdropping on the conversation.

"Indeed so," said the genderless voice in my head. Astarte 'spoke' to me the same way she now spoke to Aelia–via the implants we'd both received from Aelia's people, which Astarte could telekinetically manipulate as easily as the convincing lifelike replica of a snake poised like a statue on the end of my bed. "I am aware that the commander of the force that believes itself in control of this place has given you a deadline to provide certain items we need to discuss.

"I'm also aware that you have been confined to this cell until that deadline arrives. Was breaking that man's nose truly necessary?"

"Probably not," I said. "Although he may think twice the next time he decides to interrupt a private conversation."

"Doubtful," said Astarte.

"What else do you know? Can you tell me anything about that vehicle moored next to the temple compound?"

"Little, probably, that you could not have guessed at. It uses technology much like I recall of Aelia's people, but in ways I have not seen before–including modifications that seem to have been made by humans."

"What about their enslaved Selenite?" I asked.

"That is no more their own doing than that vehicle. I have no prior knowledge of Aelia's people doing such a thing, but it would seem they have found a better use for Selenites than merely eradicating them."

"The 'Selenite' might think otherwise," Case said.

"What a species that harvests worlds might think of enslavement is not my concern, construct," Astarte replied. "Nor would it be yours, if you had not been made from something *they* made."

"So... you know about Real Me?" Case asked.

"I know only that the image in Murphy's implant is not of a normal human brain. Knowing what I know of Selenites, what seems most likely is that the original you were recorded from was a human hybrid they created.

"I find it odd that you would feel sympathy for the creatures that made you such a thing. But you seem to be more human than not–and humans are often foolish in their sympathies. Does the creature's suffering concern you?"

"Her name," Case said, "Is Celeste."

"Selenites have no need of names, construct," Astarte said. "As they have no individual consciousness. But, by all means, call the creature whatever you prefer."

"You're wrong," Case said. "When they enslaved her, they broke her from her hive. She doesn't *want* to be an individual, any more than she wants to be a slave–could you help her?"

"I could end her suffering as easily as I could end yours," Astarte said. "I considered it from the moment the creature was brought to this world."

“Why didn’t you?” I asked.

“Much the same reason I tolerated *you*, Murphy. The novelty of your existence entertains me. Now I have a question for you... if I may.”

“Of course.”

“There is a small mountain near this place. There is a cave near that mountain’s summit. That place has been my secret since before your kind evolved. How did you know of it?”

It was a confirmation, not a question, and we both knew it. It might have been a test of how much I was willing to trust the data ghost in my head. Whatever the reason, I had no problem answering.

“I told you when I got here that I had known both yours and Aelia’s counterpart on my own Earth–that may seem unlikely... but it’s true.

“What I *didn’t* tell you was that your counterpart rewarded me with that cave, among other things, for services rendered. Have you been able to examine the artifacts I left there?”

“My senses are not as keen over distances as they once were,” Astarte said. “Those ‘artifacts’ contain something so close to the stuff of my own being that I can *easily* imagine that a being able to sense such things–say, for example, an enslaved Selenite–might confuse one for the other.”

“Or confuse either,” I said, “with something called ‘wellesium’ that apparently is used on some other Earth to float airships.”

“Or that.”

“I’m being candid with you,” I said. “So I’m going to ask for some candor in return.”

"In what way," said the genderless voice in my head, "do you feel I have been less than candid?"

"Just one, so far–but it's a pretty big one. It is not merely your *senses* that have weakened over distance... is it?"

"You are bold, Murphy. Please continue."

"I'm bold when I know I'm *right*," I said, *really* hoping I was right. "Do I think you could 'strike me down' right now? Yeah, I do–if you can sense and manipulate the junk in my head at the level required to create the 'voice' I'm hearing, you could *easily* stop my heart–or cause a brain aneurysm, or whatever.

"Could you have done the same thing from a distance–say, when I first touched down on the far side of the continent? I don't think so. I think you're running a bluff. If you could just whack these guys strutting around your private property with rayguns... I think you would've done it already–I don't think you're keeping *them* alive for your amusement.

"I think you've weakened to the point that you can no longer manipulate matter at any real distance, no longer see matter in extreme detail at any real distance, and that everything you do weakens you–and hastens the day that you're little more than an inert remnant from the dawn of time."

"You are more correct than not," said the voice in my head. "Although I caution you that it is not in either of our interests to test the limits of my abilities. Another question, Murphy: what was the service you did my counterpart to deserve such rewards?"

"I helped him obtain the one thing he truly wanted," I said. "I helped him leave Earth. The last time we spoke, he was on his way to the center of creation... determined to once again commune with God."

“That communion would be brief,” Astarte said, “since traveling to the center of creation would require effectively all time left in creation... even for an angel.”

For a long time after that, the voice in my head remained silent. The semblance of a serpent coiled next to me remained statue-still. I was beginning to wonder if I had finally exhausted my entertainment value when the voice finally spoke again.

“If another version of me saw fit to trust you,” Astarte said, “I shall trust you as well. I cannot reward you with things to which you have already been entrusted–but I will ask that you ensure, if you can, that the faith Aelia and her acolytes have placed in me is kept.

“Will you do that, Murphy?”

“If I can.”

“I believe you... and I thank you.

“Now, let us see if we can use the time that remains to determine a way that you can complete your mission.”

“In two days,” I said, “Wolfreich plans to start executing hostages if I don’t give him what he wants–starting with you and Aelia.”

The serpent coiled at the foot of my bed couldn’t smile, of course, but I could hear the smile in the voice in my head. “And that is why you and I are going to give him *precisely* what he wants.”

## seven: kayce

“Just how long is this... procedure going to continue?”

“Mr. Ellsberg agreed to up to a full twenty four hours, Captain Cullen. We're coming up on fourteen hours now.”

"And how do we know this is accomplishing *anything*?"

"He's been talking his head off for the last two hours. Most of it doesn't make any sense–but we're recording it all."

"That sounds like normal behavior for anyone in his situation. If he was experiencing something... out of the ordinary, how would we know?"

"We'd see a shift in his vitals, maybe he'd teleport himself out of the tank."

"Is that what you're expecting, Sr. Hardin?"

"Not really," Charlie Hardin said. "But you have to admit... It would be *really* cool."

I sighed. Maybe Hiram Díaz really *had* 'gotten away with it' yet again.

Hardin was a civilian contractor for Texas Air Corps, which meant he answered to General Bush, not me. But if anything happened to Saul... I was going to find a way to make them *both* pay.

We were in a hangar on the far side of the airfield from the building my team operated out of. In front of me was a clear tube filled with liquid. Suspended in that tube, a figure in a black, skin-tight suit that covered him entirely, including the face. An air supply tube attached where the mouth would be. The limbs floated free in the liquid and twitched occasionally.

Charlie Hardin was maybe all of thirty-five. An engineer on long-term loan from Hughes Aircraft Corporation, he supposedly knew more about the restored vehicle called 'Ghost One' than anyone else. He'd also figured out how to accelerate the 'repair' of Ghost One's nonhuman pilot.

"It would be *completely* cool," I told him. "But I don't think it's going to happen. Meanwhile, you are subjecting a California citizen to extreme enhanced interrogation techniques."

"He agreed to do this," Hardin said.

"And I'm still responsible for him. If there are any long-term consequences to this... I am going to make you pay."

Hardin gulped. "Understood."

* * *

"When I first met you and Mr. Ellsberg, he looked like someone who'd just figured out that mixin' raw mescal and ether's a bad idea–not that I'd know anything about that *personally*, of course."

My orders included a routine 'one on one' meeting with General Bush. Since I was the ranking RCN officer–actually, the *only* officer–attached to the joint project, it was something I had to do.

I'd thought about rescheduling it until after Saul's isolation tank session, then thought about it again. If this was going to turn out badly, I needed the Texicans to understand just how bad it was going to be.

We were sitting in Bush's office on the top floor of his main headquarters building, at a break table in the corner of the office. Through the windows, I could see the airfield stretching out toward the adjacent commercial field: Hughes Aerodrome. In the distance, I could see the taller buildings of San Antonio.

"As I recall," I said, "you offered him oxygen, b-complex vitamins, and thorazine. Not on the basis of *personal* experience... of course."

"Now, *that's* what I'm talkin' about," Bush said with a grin and a wink. "Hiram said you'd be good at this... he was right."

"I appreciate the admiral's confidence," I said. "As well as your candor.

"I need to be equally candid, sir. This is a temporary assignment I did *not* want, dealing with matters I would prefer to have as little to do with as possible. But I have responsibilities, and I intend to keep them. We need to talk about Sr. Ellsberg."

"Yes, Captain, I expect we do. Where would you like to start?"

"I'd say we start with the obvious: a California citizen is currently undergoing extreme enhanced interrogation at the hands of Texas Air Corps defense contractors under your direct supervision.

"The fact that this citizen consented to this treatment is of *no consequence* if he experiences lasting damage as a result of this. I'm formally providing notice, as required, that I intend to take official action if this turns out to be the case."

"I would expect nothing less, Captain–but here's the deal: you've already submitted a report to your own Admiralty outlinin' *multiple* occasions when you believed that Saul Ellsberg was either a direct or contributin' cause to some... fairly non-standard stuff."

"I was under the impression," I interrupted, "That I was delivering that report over a secured *private* channel."

"That's correct, Captain–and I requested a copy of the report as soon as you gave it. Most of it's redacted as hell, but there's a few things that stick out–namely, that both you and Hiram Díaz *believe* that Mr. Ellsberg had a role in these events.

"As it happens, I think so as well–because we have corroboratin' evidence from a source of our own: 'Ghost One,' my old buddy and your new friend... Ruhl Skattersmythe."

"If you accept this as evidence," I said, "Then why are your people using extreme methods to obtain more?"

"Because I *need* more, Captain, and you damn well know it. Ruhl says a *lot* of things. You got a pretty fair earful when I took y'all out to meet him. What did *you* think?"

I had been trying to process that meeting ever since it occurred. Ruhl Skattersmythe was humanoid, not human, claimed to be over five hundred years old, and claimed that almost everything I thought I knew about history was wrong.

He'd told me his species had secretly ruled my world for thousands of years–until what he called a '*demiurgos'* had cast them out. He also said that the 'thunderbolts' that had brought down his ship and the craft later taken by Yanquis had been thrown by the same *demiurgos*–who conveniently seemed to have lost that power sometime in the last fifty years.

Thanks to the Texicans, he was 'alive' again, but a lot of things about his resurrection... seemed to have gone awry. What looked like machinery intended to support Ruhl's life was now essentially *part* of him.

"If he was *human*," I replied, "I'd say he was unhinged. Possibly he is anyway."

"Trust me, Captain," Bush said. "I *know* the feeling. After being 'mostly dead' and buried for the better part of a century, it's safe to say the boy ain't right–but here's the thing: on his good days... you can kinda tell what

Ruhl must've been like before he got killed. As far as *he's* concerned... we're pretty much just cavemen.

"On his *really* good days... Ruhl scares the *shit* out of me. And anything that scares *him* is something you and I had better take very, *very* seriously."

"So... what are you really hoping to accomplish here, General?"

"Honestly, Captain Cullen, I'm not even sure. After Charlie read the report on Mr. Ellsberg, he suggested this and Ellsberg agreed. Worst-case scenario is that Ellsberg winds up back in therapy–hell, I'll even foot the bill. Best case is that he comes outta that tank with *something* we can use."

# Part 3: Demiurge, Archangels, & Alien

## *one: ellsberg*

I'd heard of 'isolation tank therapy' before. There were boutiques all over San Francisco where you could microdose on psilocybin, get plopped into a tank, and have a visionary experience. Nice, I suppose, if you could afford it. Being of more modest means and already having problems with 'visionary experiences,' I'd never been inclined to try it... before now.

Only I wouldn't exactly describe what I was experiencing as 'therapy.'

Once upon a time, Yanquis inquisitors had used this technique to squeeze information out of people. Civilized countries didn't do such things, but the literature on it was pretty widely available... and the Texicans just happened to have a leftover tank that was pretty well perfect for it.

I could *totally* understand how it worked for 'enhanced interrogation.'

The suit I was in completely negated any sense of touch, any light, any smell. The breathing apparatus built into the suit's hood fed me air and allowed me to talk, but my ears were plugged against *any* sound. Vibrations through my bones fed a faint whisper of my own voice... but that was all.

After a time, time becomes meaningless. At first it's just boring, but then it's terrifying–all too easy to imagine that you have been buried alive or forgotten. All too easy to imagine that this is what *death* is like–a brain cut off from everything except the awareness of itself... in the last few moments before, even *that* is taken away.

Except, unlike death, the moment went on and on.

Eventually, you start hallucinating. Starved of stimulus, your brain invents its own. People undergoing this have claimed to remember long-lost childhood memories, or even memories of past lives. I'd settle for an actual memory of my own life–adult *or* child–before it had been interfered with.

Before *they* came.

Helene had *almost* gotten me there with hypnosis. I can remember wandering in San Francisco in the cold, not even knowing who I was. My wallet told me I was 'Saul Ellsberg' and told me where 'Saul Ellsberg' lived. When I finally found the apartment, the keys in my pocket let me in.

But I still didn't know I was *me*.

That came later, and it was hard as hell. By that time, the dreams had started happening. I *think* I now know what happened–what did it to me, maybe even *why*.

But I still don't remember it.

If nothing came of this and I actually got out of this tank, that skinny little Texican engineer and I were going to have some words. I detest violence and I always have... but suffering through this for nothing was unthinkable.

Then... in the darkness... *something*.

The specks of light came in from the periphery of my vision, swirling about themselves in a spiral. Then more of them,

Then more.

“That’s not *really* what I see,” said a familiar voice. “You have a human brain. The extra colors and dimensions are lost on you. But you should at least grasp the scale.”

“Am I looking at a galaxy?” I said.

“Close enough,” said Colvin Case.

* * *

The first time, he’d shown me a hellish cityscape in what he assured me was just some other version of Texas. The second time, it had been a battle of starships, as seen from the surface of the moon. Both had been dreams, sort of–was this one as well?

Thinning hair, tinted glasses, expensive tailoring–he looked the same as he had before. The table he and I had sat at the last time was the same, whether on a balcony overlooking a hellscape or the edge of a lunar crater. Realizing I once again had a sense of touch, I touched my own chest and looked down. Chinos, oxford shirt, rumpled jacket–not a skin tight rubber suit.

“Am I dreaming?” I asked.

“Not any more than the last time,” Case said. “Scoot your chair over a bit–I’ve asked someone to join us.”

I did as he asked, taking in the scene around me as I did. We were on a cobbled stone courtyard. Across from us: a stepped stone pyramid that I recognized as a Mayan temple. Over the temple hung the galaxy, or whatever it was, lighting the scene as bright as the brightest full moon.

Once I had moved my chair away from Case, the space I’d been in acquired another chair and an occupant. A slight, pretty, blonde woman with large blue eyes, wearing a gray cocktail dress, dark tights, and flats. "Hello," she said. "I'm Celeste. Good to see you again."

"I don't remember having had the pleasure," I said.

"If any of us had our *true* appearance," Case said, "this would be far less pleasant–especially for *me*." He gestured like a man getting a waiter's attention. Like the last time, a waiter appeared from nowhere. "Celeste doesn't drink, but I know you do–so I took the liberty of ordering a scotch for you."

The waiter set drinks before us and then conveniently vanished.

"You're currently on the receiving end of some treatment Celeste and I both know very, very well–with the significant difference that you *agreed* to it and shortly get decanted... we're not so lucky. On the other hand, it's a *lot* easier to jack you up to our speed while your body's in that tank. That's a *good* thing... we've got a lot to cover."

I looked at Celeste again. There was something about the eyes. "I remember now. You were screaming."

"Part of me screams all the time," Celeste said. "You heard it... Because of what was done to you."

"And then I got away from it–can you tell me how?"

"I am a slave," she replied. "Forcibly separated from my kind, lost in the dark until Case found me. I know that my people made you into a tool to access a world previously closed to them. Once they found a way back into your world... they no longer needed you. But the abilities they gave you could still be used."

"Used by *who*? And how is it that we are even talking? That's never happened before."

"That would be *my* doing," Case said. "*All* of it, actually. That screaming you heard in your mind? I heard it as well. My mind is enough like hers that we can share thoughts... just not *human* thoughts.

"I heard you as well, Saul. You screamed when they ripped you away from your world, you screamed when they put that thing in your head. I *know* that pain. The only reason you aren't both hearing *me* scream... is that I screamed myself silent years ago."

"Why *me*?" I said. "Can you at least tell me that? No one else can."

"My people are not cruel," Celeste said. "You were just in the right place and time for what they needed. The same is true of how *you* were born, Case. What happened to you later, cruel or not... was inflicted by other humans."

"The fucking Space Elfs are *not* human," Case said. "And I *really* don't want to talk about that."

"What *do* you want to talk about?" I asked. "Is this really happening, or am I just having one seriously detailed hallucination?"

"A little bit of both," Case said. "I'm able to stick the important bits in your head and tag Celeste into the call. Your imagination takes it from there. Actually, *you* called *me*–but the timing was good... I needed to set something like this up, anyway."

"I'm listening," I said.

"There is about to be a *very* narrow window of opportunity for *everyone* to get what they want." Case said. "An old friend of mine is about to deliver some very powerful goods. They aren't *exactly* what he was told they were, but that doesn't matter. Whatever he does is going to involve a fairly massive energy release... that I have plans for."

“What if he doesn’t do anything?” I asked.

“That’s not going to be an available option. Also, it’s not his style. He’ll wind up doing *something*.

“When he does, assuming you do your part, Celeste & I get free–well, sort of–in exchange for which, the people you’re working for get *all* the information they want on alien technology they’ve pissed away fifty years trying to understand. They get the most highly qualified ‘subject matter experts’ imaginable... *us*.

“I can even throw in a non-crashed UFO–assuming your people can put some boots on the ground to take it.

“*You*,” he continued, “get out from under. The Greys threw you away as soon as they realized they didn’t need you. You’ve been *my* asset ever since–and don’t hold your breath waiting for an apology. My position on the fucked-over scale is *way* ahead of yours. But if you help me pull this off, I’ll get that thing out of your head and send you on your way... free and clear. Sound good?”

“Maybe,” I said. “It depends on what you need me to do. But there’s some shit *I* need, Case.”

“Like what?”

“Right now, I’m in an isolation tank tripping my balls off–and the main reason I’m there is because the ‘people I work for’ need some hard data that you aren’t a figment of my imagination. They need *proof* before they are going to do anything.”

“I can arrange that,” Case said. “What else?”

“I need you to level with me. That shit that started happening when I left San Francisco–that’s *all* you... isn’t it?”

Case smiled and waved the imaginary waiter back into existence long enough to top off our imaginary drinks. “Yeah, pretty much. The Greys used you to find out if it was safe to visit your world again. Once they had that, they were done with you.

“Once they are done, they are *really* done. That chip in your head would’ve degraded into random bits of protein if I hadn’t hijacked it.”

“And that’s not *all* you ‘hijacked’... is it?”

Case shrugged. “You were no use to me in a pile of wreckage on the side of a mountain. When the ship you were traveling in came under attack, I moved it.”

“Three times, apparently. Under attack by *who*?”

“Not by ‘who,’ by *‘what’*,” he said. “They were called ‘foo fighters’ when they first showed up on my world–but that’s just a name. I think of them as organic flying drones, but that’s probably not going to mean much to you. They can interfere with electrical power systems... but you already know that.”

“So these things just happened to be flying around and decided to attack my airship?”

“They can be trained,” Celeste said. “My people have used them, so have others. But this could just be a wild flock that wandered into your skies from elsewhen. I don’t know.”

“And what about what happened at the Majestic Conference? Same thing, right?”

“Pretty much,” Case replied. “I needed you to be free to act. I also needed you to be where you are right now.”

"In *Texas*?"

"Yeah, I know. Not my favorite place, either. But the version you're in has assets we can use."

"If you can arrange something like that," I said. "Why do you need me at all?"

"I have limits," he said. "The more I directly intervene in your world, the more it costs me. I can't pull this off without you."

"I still need *proof* of all this," I said. "Otherwise, I'm probably going to wind up pretty damned useless–unless you can snatch me out before a bunch of Texicans decide to take a buzzsaw to my head."

He chuckled dryly. "That's not going to happen. We're going to make it worth their while to play along. Still got that piece of paper I gave you?"

I checked my jacket pocket. "It's still not real," I said.

"Take it out and look at it."

I did. It looked like a piece of paper torn from a notebook. Scrawled on it were half a dozen sets of numbers and dates, in what looked like my handwriting. "What the hell is this?"

"It's every place Murphy has spent more than 24 hours at a time since he got dropped into your world–write it out when you get out, tell your new buddies to check it out."

"Who the hell is 'Murphy'?" I asked.

"Even with you jacked up to my speed, that's a little longer story than I want to get into," Case replied. "Let's just say he's an old friend on the receiving end of a long con... and you, Celeste, and I are going to cash in on the payoff."

"Assuming I'm onboard, what exactly do you need me to do?"

"There's a parcel with your name on it sitting in 'will call' in the central post office in Dallas, Texas. It will tell you everything you need to know."

Dallas? It *couldn't* be... but it would explain a lot. "Those fanzines–they came from *you.*"

He chuckled again. "Correct, old buddy. What's in that *last* parcel should answer any and all questions anyone has about whether or not I'm 'real'."

"What if it doesn't? What if they still don't buy it?"

"After this, it's all on you. I'm going to be laying low, conserving what I've got left for the big finale. If there's anything else you need... you'd best ask for it now."

"Do you realize how much this smells like a scam?" I asked. On a whim, I raised my glass and waggled it. Case's imaginary waiter obediently materialized, topped off my drink, and vanished again. "First, there's a 'need for urgency' that *can't* be verified. Then there's the fact that everyone who seems to know anything about what's *really* going on talks about it in metaphors and allusions. Can you guys *please* just tell me what the actual fuck any of this is?"

"You need to give Celeste a break," Case said. "She's still learning how to think human. So is that poor bastard zombie space elf you ran into. Meanwhile, she's teaching me how to think like a Grey... more or less."

"And what is *that* like?"

"Disturbing," he said. "There are times when I'm not sure whether I *found* your world or *created* it. I'm pretty sure I know how *I* was created. Other times... not so much.

"'Metaphor and allusion' is what humans turn to when 'the actual fuck' is either too complex or too bloody awful–so do nonhumans, for that matter. It was easiest for me to just cut to the chase and offer you a deal: a working alien spaceship, mine and Celeste's combined consulting services, and your freedom... in exchange for ours."

"What's in that mail drop had better be pretty fuckin' amazing," I said.

He chuckled again, waved the waiter back into existence to top off his drink. "It's going to have to be. After this, I'm pretty much tapped out. Anything else you need?"

"Could you zap me out of the isolation tank? That would pretty much shut down *any* argument about whether or not you're real."

"It's cutting into my energy budget, and it could also go horribly wrong," Case said. "But on the other hand..."

### *two: murphy*

The serpent slithered away, leaving me to once again talk to my not so imaginary friend. He was getting increasingly glitchy, which made me wonder if there might be some sort of 'planned obsolescence' for the junk in my head... which could be a bit of a problem if it failed before I was done with it.

The ghost spoke first. "I don't like it."

"Refresh my memory on the part where you get a vote," I replied. "You're just along for the ride."

The plan we'd come up with wasn't perfect, but it was a distinct improvement over just waiting to find out if my theories about safeties on alien 'smart guns' turned out to be true. Astarte had promised to touch base with me before we hit Wolfreich's deadline for my answer on the off-chance I might've thought of something overlooked by an immortal cosmic being. While I appreciated the consideration, I didn't think it was necessary.

I knew what I was going to do.

"That ride gets cut short if you get your ass smoked trying to be a hero," Ghost Case said. "It's not like I have a lot of options."

"None whatever," I replied. "But the original version of you planned a few operations back in the day, even if he was just a desk jockey. If you don't like the plan... figure out a way to make it mo' better."

"I'll see what I can do," Case said. "But how about answering one small question first?"

"Sure–what's up?"

"Is there anything–and I do mean *anything* else you have been keeping on the downlow? Any tricks, any surprises, any other lies? You have a bad habit of treating everything and everyone on a 'need to know' basis–your wife split after she'd had enough of it, and I don't blame her. No more secrets, Murphy... *none*."

I laughed. "So says the digital ghost of a half-human dude who kept that shit so deep on the downlow that an *intelligence agency* actually promoted him to management."

"*Not* a good comparison; Real Me believed he was human all along. Meanwhile, you were a double agent at the same agency–and absolutely knew *exactly* what you were... even if no one else ever did."

"Point taken," I said. And I had to admit that he was right. I *do* operate that way.

"At this point, you know everything I know. Everything I brought into this world that isn't in this room is stashed in a certain place you now know about–and I'm not going to mention out loud. As of now, you have an unqualified 'need to know' on pretty much *everything*.

"So, based on what you know–what do you not like about my plan?"

"I don't like the fact that you are *completely* counting on Astarte for something *neither* of you is certain about. What I like even less is that there is *nothing* even resembling a 'Plan B' if you are wrong."

"Sometimes, that's just how it is, Case. If you have to jump out of a plane and you don't have a backup chute... you still jump."

"Having never once jumped out of a plane with or without a backup chute, I will take your word on that one, old buddy. But there's another thing that's bothering me, and I think we need to talk about it–what about Celeste? What do you plan on doing about her?"

"Wolfreich's Grey? I plan on having as little to do with it as possible. Sorry, but I have a problem with getting tortured."

"Real Me did the same thing to you–you got over *that*."

"Not true," I said. "I just don't hold it against *you*. I'd as soon pull the plug on Case Prime as look at him–and he'd probably thank me."

"He just *might*, Murphy. But you and he were friends back when you both thought you were just human. You were friends for a long time. If you could save him... would you?"

"A bit of a pointless question," I said. "Even if I was planning on going back to our Earth, undoing what The Fortuned did to him is beyond me. He can't be saved."

"Actually, Murphy... maybe he *can*."

### *three: kayce*

"I need your professional evaluation in writing, Helene. But I also want your *personal* evaluation–which you may consider as off the record."

"Is that permitted?" We were sitting in the office the Texicans had set up for me–another of the suites in the guest house they'd given us, but equipped with a desk, filing cabinet, and a military-grade net terminal. I had *very* restricted guest access to the Texican's network, but I was able to use it to send encrypted text queries to RCN's network... and eventually receive replies. It was primitive... but I've dealt with worse.

I smiled. "I'm the ranking command grade officer on an RCN field operation–actually, the *only* one. But it means I have a certain amount of discretion. I could be ordered to recount this conversation... but it isn't likely."

Helene smiled. "As long as you are not exercising *Hiram's* levels of discretion... there should be no problem."

"Agreed," I said.

Helene had completed her examination of Saul after the abrupt end of his fifteen hour session in the Texican's jury-rigged isolation tank. She had spoken to him for over an hour. I intended to have my own session as well, after Saul–currently resting under sedation–was fully recovered. My session could wait. My evaluation of Helene's session... could not.

"Helene, I need to make a recommendation to the admiralty, a command decision of my own, and be prepared to discuss *all* of this in the next joint task force meeting. I will need your formal report for these things, but I need more than that. Let's start with the obvious: do you think what Saul is saying is true?"

"I think *he* thinks it is."

"Not good enough. Save that for your formal report. Do *you* think what Saul is telling us is real?"

She sighed, and I suddenly realized how weary she must be.

Even though I'd known Helene Abenard for the better part of a year, I'd never really known much about her. I knew she'd studied 'alien abduction' cases in private practice before Hiram Díaz had recruited her, knew that she had worked extensively with Saul over the last year trying to unravel the web of screen memories around what had happened to him, what was continuing to happen.

I knew that her and Hiram Díaz were close, and had made a point of knowing as little about *that* as possible. She was petite and precise, with large dark eyes that seemed to take in *everything*. Whatever their relationship, she'd shown Hiram Díaz loyalty I had no business expecting.

Even though I needed to ask for it, anyway.

"If you had asked me that even as recently as the day before we left San Francisco," Helene replied, "I probably would have said 'no.' I would have described Saul as someone who had made a healthy adjustment to delusions that had caused years of significant mental health issues."

"Interesting–as late as that?"

"It is not my business as Saul's therapist to weigh in on the *objective* reality of the things he claims to experience. My role has been to use hypnotherapy and other tools to help Saul recover and understand memories he could not consciously access. I've also tried to help him cope, emotionally, with how he feels personally about these things."

"And how do *you* feel about these things?"

"When Hiram first came to me for advice on these matters, I did not regard *any* of it as 'real' in any objective sense. I considered the entire business of 'mystery disks' and 'ghost airships' a recurring form of social hysteria. The fact that this hysteria seemed to be on the rise could easily be attributed to other factors–social anxiety over the possibility of war with the United States, not least of all."

"And now?"

She sighed again. "We both know what we saw, Kayce. We were on an airship that lost power and almost crashed into a mountain–and then we weren't. No one who was on the *Morrison* has an accurate or complete memory of what really happened on that trip… not even me, and I probably remember more than most.

"Then we finally made it to Dayton and the Majestic Conference… and it happened again. We were in a locked auditorium, and then we weren't–and even if Saul wasn't *directly* responsible for what happened, he was at least a conduit for it. And the only reason that you and I and Dr. Albion are even here is because that happened.

"And now… *this*. Saul's explanation of what just happened is no more fantastic than any other possible explanation. Denying the evidence of your own senses is as much a delusion as believing things for which no evidence exists, merely because you wish to believe them. I do not *want* to believe in *any* of this, Kayce–but, yes: I believe that it is true."

"Including this?" I held up the sealed plastic bag containing the piece of notebook paper Saul had given her.

"The technical name for it is 'psychography' or 'automatic writing.' It's usually associated with people who believe themselves in contact with spirits.

"When I began treating Saul, he believed that nonhuman beings communicated with him via dreams–that these beings, for reasons unknown, shared with him details of events the United States and California have been jointly investigating in secret for over fifty years. He believed that he had other dreams as well, that could be described as 'precognition'–dreams of events that would come true. There is *some* evidence this may have actually occurred.

"What Saul is now telling us is that his dreams have changed into a running dialog with someone else also connected to the nonhumans who communicate with him. He also claims that this new communicant has told him that the source of his dreams is an object embedded in his brain–an object this new communicant claims he can remove.

"My written report is going to indicate the possibility that Saul's delusions have adapted in response to being exposed to apparently real nonhumans."

"Is that what *you* believe?" I asked.

"I'm professionally obliged to mention the possibility," Helene said, "but it is *not* what I believe. We'll know soon enough if there is actually a package in Saul's name waiting at the Dallas post office. At this point, I would be more surprised if there were *not* such a package."

"DPS agents have already been sent to retrieve it, if it exists," I replied. "Agent Lochart has promised to notify me as soon as they have confirmation. I could be getting that call any minute."

"And if they find this... 'package'?"

"It goes through the same kind of forensic testing Hiram ordered for the first two 'fan pubs' Saul received in San Francisco–maybe not quite as exhaustive... I don't know if DPS equals BSI when it comes to these things.

"But even so, it is going to be tomorrow morning before this package–if it exists–winds up here. Meanwhile, DPS has already verified that half of the map coordinates Saul gave you check out against the tracking data from 'Ghost One' for this alleged intermittent ground contact–including the final contact in Central America.

"Agent Lochart has contacted DPS field offices in Texas and Oregon. She thinks she might have confirmation on those coordinates as well by early tomorrow.

"This leads me to another question, Kayce."

"Yes?" *Here it comes*, I thought.

"Saul's issues have plainly moved beyond matters of therapy. Do you *truly* need me to remain here?"

I sighed. "The short and very obvious answer is 'no.' The more obvious–and disappointing–answer is that neither one of us is free to go... not just yet."

She sighed as well. "I had expected as much. How much longer before either one of us is free to go home?"

"Technically, we are *both* required to remain until after the information-sharing agreement between Texas and California has been formalized. Realistically? I could probably cut you loose just as soon as we are no longer under 'state of emergency' conditions. That could happen just as soon as the Yanqui Presidente stops making random accusations and veiled threats of war."

"In other words," Helene replied, "I should plan to be here for a while."

I sighed. "*You're* a trained psychiatrist–you tell me."

### *four: murphy*

The diagram hanging in the air in front of me looked a lot like the schematics Case–the *real* one–used to scribble on yellow legal pads, back in the old days when we would get high and find backdoors on secure systems–in our free time, for the hell of it.

It didn't surprise me that Ghost Case was at least as good at building network diagrams as Case Prime, or that he'd figured out a way to do it without a legal pad and a bump of cocaine. The diagram he was building in the air was a bit surprising, but it shouldn't have been.

It wasn't like either one of them had anything better to do.

"All he can do is sense your location relative to the Dawn Matter he sensed in the first place," Ghost Case said. "He can't access your mind, and neither can I... get *over* it."

"I am... pretty much. What about 'Celeste'?"

"Same thing. Since she–to use *your* term–'mindfucked' you, she is aware of your location... and that's it."

"For now," I said, "let's assume I believe you. What about," I pointed to the diagram, "*this* part?"

"That's the bidirectional feed between Real Me and Celeste. Since I don't have an organic brain, I don't get to be a part of that."

“Or at least, so you say,” I replied. I pointed to a different part of the diagram. “What about *this*?”

“That’s how I got into Celeste’s mind while she had you locked down. It’s pretty much unidirectional, even though she knew I was there.”

“Again, I’m going to take you at your word on this for now. How about explaining this part?” I said, pointing to a dotted line between the network node labeled ‘real me’ and the one labeled ‘fake me.’

“That’s the part I wasn’t going to tell you about,” Case said. “But now I *have* to.”

* * *

I guess I shouldn’t be too surprised that a guy who was half Grey Alien would be *really good* at hacking. The Greys have had their own versions of computers and networks since dinosaurs were still alive. Their hiveminds merged with their own data networks before humanity ever evolved.

That’s part of the reason communicating with them is virtually impossible. They’re so immersed in their own data systems they’re incapable of seeing past them.

That... and the fact that they normally don’t bother talking to the livestock.

The *only* reason I’d been recruited for this gig in the first place was because I was on the short list of people Case Prime had ever mindfucked–and I was the only one who either had or could be trained into the necessary skills for a mission like this.

An artificial wormhole had been generated, at no small expense, between this version of Earth and mine. Mere molecules wide, kept open with the entire output of a secret geothermal plant in Greenland, it was good for one thing–and one thing only: sending an encoded signal with the relative location of two objects in this world: me, and the 'dawn matter' I'd been sent to either return to God or drop into a black hole.

I had been assured repeatedly when I took this gig that the *only* thing coming through the data feed was the location data. I was also assured that the feed was unidirectional, and I believed it, given the energy requirements. Unless I wanted to get hooked up to a nuclear reactor… *nothing* was going the other way.

But Case Prime was a crafty bastard, and the lab in Greenland where he was slowly mutating into a pile of sentient goo offered few entertainments. He'd hacked his way into another system, one with a little more bandwidth, and uploaded a copy of himself into my implants.

That system had shut down the moment the survey ship that brought me here had entered the rift between worlds, but by then it didn't matter. I hadn't been particularly happy about finding a copy of the son of a bitch in my head, but I got used to it. 'Ghost Case' was useful, and I could switch him off if he got too annoying.

Like now, for example.

* * *

"You said you weren't going to get mad," Case sulked.

"I'm not mad," I said. "Just… surprised. And I don't even understand how this is possible. Evangeia told me the data feed just went one way."

"Sure," Case said. "And it *does*. Look at the diagram again. Real Me and Celeste have a bidirectional connection. I have a unidirectional connection with Celeste. Real Me has a unidirectional connection with

Fake Me. It's a little cumbersome... but it still means we can all communicate."

"I was also told," I said, "that the feed through the wormhole had just enough bandwidth for the location data–and nothing more."

"Who do you think is better at this?" Ghost Case asked. "*Me*, or your Space Elf girlfriend? Yeah, it's a tight connection–but it's not like we have anything better to do. And you should be glad." He added some lines to the diagram. "If we hadn't hacked the system, we wouldn't be able to talk to *this* guy!"

I looked at the diagram. "What the fuck is a 'Saul Ellsberg'?"

"Someone else with a history of getting fucked over by Greys, someone else who wants to get out from under. He's got an implant–not like *yours*, it's the stuff Greys do–and Real Me figured out how to hack into it."

"And this gets us... what?"

"It doesn't get *you* anything–but it isn't always about *you*, Murphy. It gets Real Me and Celeste a way out."

"Would you be able to *join* them?"

The digital ghost laughed. "Finally, had enough of my shit, old buddy? Can't say that I blame you. Actually, that *might* be possible–but first we need to take care of them."

"And what does this Ellsberg guy get?"

"Out from under. Real Me promised to remove his implant."

"He can *do* that?"

"He can do it all exactly *once*–that's why the timing on this has to be *perfect*."

"Asking me to trust 'real you'," I said, "is a pretty big fucking ask, you know."

He chuckled dryly. "I know that better than anyone. Oh, and speaking of 'asks', here's another: tell Astarte to stop shooting down drones."

"What the fuck does that–"

And, since timing is pretty much *everything*, I wasn't exactly surprised when a blinking dot painted itself into the corner of my vision and a neutral, genderless voice said "Incoming call."

I touched the command stud beneath the skin behind my left ear and muttered "Social interface off." As Case disappeared, I kept my finger on the stud and said, "Accept call."

Everything else in my vision went wherever Case goes, and I began to wonder if I had made a bad impulse judgment call.

Then the world rebuilt itself.

I was standing on the dais topping the pyramid I'd once heard called 'Fire Within' in a troubling dream–except I wasn't really there, for a full moon hung in the sky on what had been a moonless night.

She was facing away from me, dressed in the same plain linen robe she'd worn when The Sisters of The Commune had brought me before her, her deep dark red hair bound in a plait on her shoulder.

Without turning, she spoke. "I know that Astarte counsels you, has told you much. Before it is too late... we must speak as well."

"Nice office," I said.

"I *hate* it," Kayce replied. "I appreciate the Texicans making us comfortable, but all it *really* says to me is that this 'temporary assignment' could wind up lasting a long, long time. Evaluating what the Texicans are sharing with us is going to take time, time that I would prefer to be spending with my wife. Did I mention that I'd been planning to resign?"

"You may've mentioned it once or twice."

She was sitting behind a desk piled with papers, wearing a flight suit and an exasperated expression. I had a feeling I'd contributed to that exasperation... but I wasn't sure there was much I could do about it. "My wife mentions it every time I ever talk to her. She would like me to come home–so would I."

"Well, since you mention it, I'm pretty well done with Texas myself."

"The only person who is particularly happy with this is Dr. Albion. She's in Aurora right now with Charley Hardin. We'll be hearing from them in the joint staff meeting later today. I'm sure she'll have a lot to share."

"After finally having a chance to talk to an actual space alien?" I said. "No doubt."

"*You*, on the other hand, talk to them all the time–and you and I need to talk about that."

"Yeah... *that*. Where do we start?"

She picked up a sheaf of typewritten pages. "This is a transcript of everything you said while you were in the tank. I also have a transcript of

Helene's interview with you after you... let's just say 'ended the session.' I also have Helene's formal report–which I'm sitting on until after I have one from you as well.

"We also have a set of map coordinates and timestamps that apparently mark out every single place this so-called 'intermittent ground target' has spent any time since apparently getting dropped off by a spaceship on the Oregon coast–a list *you* wrote as soon as you were able." She sighed. "And–of course–the list checks out.

"Finally," she said, "There is the latest installment in the series of anonymous fan publications you've been receiving in the mail–although I guess we can stop calling them 'anonymous.' Apparently... it beats the first two all to hell."

"It was really there?" I asked.

"Oh, yes," Kayce replied. "'*Demiurge, Archangels, and Aliens*' is currently undergoing analysis at a DPS forensics lab. We'll have copies of it by later today, as well as the forensics report... but you and I already know what that report is going to say."

"Yeah, pretty much," I said. "I guess he's real, then."

"Your imaginary friend who claims to be half-alien? Don't be surprised if the admiralty has some abiding skepticism on that."

"What about *you*?" I asked.

She dropped the transcript and Helene's report on her desk and sighed. "I honestly don't know *what* to think, Saul. I taught history for a living before Hiram Díaz roped me into all this. I *don't* believe in 'conspiracies' without a good reason. I *do* believe in applying logical analysis to data from any source–whether it's Balkan troop movements or the claims of a mediocre writer with known substance abuse issues... sorry, but that's how the Admiralty Council tends to see you."

"No offense taken."

She laughed. "Compared to what they are saying about Hiram Díaz, that's *nothing*. The problem is this: no matter how unorthodox Admiral Díaz's methods or theories might be, no matter how bizarre your claims and experience get... you both keep *getting it right*.

"I've watched the entire world go crazy for most of the last year. Reports of unexplained aerial phenomena have become so commonplace they don't even make the news anymore. I've watched the Yanqui government devolve into a personality cult that believes a third-rate country somehow has the means to turn the entire western hemisphere into a dangerously unstable man's personal empire... well, maybe they *do*."

"Or maybe they are just being played," I said. "So far, it's all just talk."

"Or not," Kayce replied. "And that's the problem. All we *really* know is whatever has been happening for the last year has both accelerated and changed over the last *month*.

"Instead of wondering whether or not the Yanquis have broken their end of the Majestic Agreement, we're wondering whether or not they're receiving military assistance from even *worse* Yanquis from another universe.

"Instead of wondering whether or not extradimensional alien intruders are even possible, we're trying to figure out why, exactly, an alien intruder has been traveling cross country on a motorcycle, picking fights with small town cops, and apparently spending one *hell* of a lot of time hanging out in libraries."

"I *think* I might know the answer to that one," I said.

"You probably do," she replied. "Unfortunately, *you're* part of the problem as well. I don't know how the admiralty is going to react when I tell them you just 'teleported'–that's the word, right?"

"It'll do."

"You just teleported *again*, this time in front of cameras and witnesses, including members of the Texas Air Force, DPS Special Operations, and a handful of Texan and Californiano defense contractors. Once I deliver my next report, any remaining skepticism about what Admiral Díaz and I have both claimed happened at Dayton... is gone. The only real question remains what, exactly, the admiralty wants to do with you."

"I'm guessing," I said, "that finishing up my contract here isn't an option."

"Actually," she replied, "it *might* be. It all comes down to a question of where the admiralty sees the most value to California. I'm not going to make a report *or* a recommendation until after I see this latest 'fan publication' and the forensic analysis."

She picked up Helene's report. "I have a fair idea from *this* what you're proposing. If the Texicans are willing to go along with it, I *might* be able to sell it to the admiralty–but no promises. And if I get orders to send you back to California for detailed medical testing... that's *exactly* what I am going to do."

### *six: murphy*

She turned to face me, standing on that temple dais that wasn't really there. "I have not done this in a long time," Aelia said. "With my people gone... there was no need."

Even though I knew it was an illusion projected into my implants, I was still amazed by how much and how little she resembled the half-human woman who had seduced me into serving the same inhuman masters. The same magenta hair, the same blue eyes, the same dusting of freckles I'd somehow managed to not notice for almost fifty years.

Of course the same, for they *were* the same. Born of a human mother and a father from the race that call themselves 'The Fortuned,' the differences between 'Aelia' and 'Evangeia' were differences of choice and circumstance–and not merely their own choices.

Those differences had created worlds. In this world, a fallen archangel had taken the form of the goddess 'Astarte' out of love for the woman before me, had become this world's protector, driving away all the alien others who might otherwise exploit it.

In my world, that same fallen immortal had been as indifferent to humankind as any average human would be to an infestation of rodents. If the being I eventually came to know as 'Morningstar' had ever loved anything besides the god he had fallen away from... he did a pretty good job of concealing it–and certainly no love between him and the woman I knew as 'Evangeia d'Lordes.' They regarded each other with little more than amused contempt.

"I've never placed one of these calls at all," I replied. "My list of acquaintances with this sort of hardware is pretty short."

"From what you have said, I gather that list includes an alternative version of myself."

"It does, but almost as soon as she managed to get me equipped with this gear, it was time to send me here. We didn't chat much after that."

She arched a single perfect eyebrow, a gesture I remember well. “I dare say.”

“To what do I owe the pleasure?” I asked. “Did you just want to make sure the hardware still worked?”

“Hardly. I know somewhat of what Astarte is planning with you. I should prefer to know more.”

“Fair,” I said, wondering what I was getting myself into. I did *not* want to get in the middle of a lover’s quarrel between a grounded archangel and her consort.

A further question was also forming in my mind. Astarte had given me the impression that Aelia was experiencing some sort of cognitive decline. What an angel defines as early onset dementia could still be super-genius level by human standards–at least, for all I knew.

I was going to have to play this *very* carefully.

“I have other questions as well,” she said, “starting with the obvious.” She pointed to my shoulder. “Do you *truly* understand the significance of that mark you bear? I must be sure.”

I’d received it the same day I’d received the cybernetic implant that made this conversation possible. More than just a tattoo, it symbolized an obligation I’d accepted. If it didn’t mean what I thought it meant, best I’d be finding that out *now*.

“Your counterpart bore it as well, insisted to her elders that I receive it. It means that I am part of what your kind call ‘The Obligate.’ It means that I have accepted an obligation to serve your people. It means as well that The Obligate will retrieve me when this mission is done... if I want it.”

“It is more complex than that,” she said. “But you are essentially correct. Even so, do not assume my father’s folk do not find subtle and self-serving ways to interpret such obligations. *Your* father’s folk as well? Or was it your mother?”

“Neither. I was an old and dying man, a human. Your people gave me a serum that made me younger and made me like you.”

“Then you must have done, or are intended to do, something fairly remarkable. Such gifts are not lightly bestowed.”

“More the latter, I think,” I replied. “Has Astarte told you what I was charged to deliver?”

“She suspects you are intended to either restore or destroy her. She also thinks she can use these ‘gifts’ as she pleases… irrespective their original intent.”

“What we have planned depends upon that. Do you believe her?”

She smiled. “I believe that my beloved is several billions years more aged than to be either overconfident or ill-informed. But she has made mistakes before. If she is making another… it could go badly for you.”

“I’m prepared to accept that,” I said. “My time in your world has been short, but long enough to believe that it is worth preserving.”

“Forgive this, if it is presumption… but did you not feel the same of your own world?”

I join her at the edge of the dais. Beneath us, we could see the fires and homes of *La Comuna de las Hermanas.* In the distance, silvered by the moonlight, we could see the towering trees of the rainforest that surrounded us. I felt an incredible sense of peace.

"Not really," I said. "My world has been exploited and abused repeatedly, by your counterpart among others... and I played no small role in the abuse. I accept what I did, but I will do it no more. I will die to preserve this world–not what I want, but I will do as I must."

"As will I," she said, reaching out to me in the perfect illusion of that night.

I had not expected the embrace, but I accepted it. Real or not, was I transgressing on a relationship I could barely understand?

Maybe... But I always trust my instincts.

And my instincts said... *yes*.

## seven: kayce

"Am I to understand, Captain, that you are buyin' into *any* of this?"

"General, I have been asking myself variations of that question ever since Admiral Díaz recruited me. Until recently, the answer was not just 'no'... but hell, no."

As the ranking officer for the California Navy part of the joint task force, I was more or less obligated to have a routine personal touch base with General Bush. Having it before the meeting with the entire task force had seemed like a good idea.

Particularly *this* meeting.

"So what changed ya?"

"When the theories that met all the facts that did *not* admit the fantastic became more convoluted than the ones that did."

Bush chuckled and nodded. "Same, Captain. I didn't actually believe a word of this 'aliens' bullcrap myself until I met ol' Ruhl–and you've seen a fair chunk more of this than I have–did Ellsberg *really* jump an airship over a mountain... just by thinking about it?"

"I no longer think Saul actually did *anything*. I think something else uses him as a... let's say a 'targeting system.' Is he the *reason* it happened? Yes–I do think that."

"Ruhl seems to think the same thing, even if he don't say it quite the same way."

"Then there's what happened in Dayton. No one really saw it happen, but my entire team disappeared from a locked auditorium and reappeared at a party you were throwing in a nearby hotel. I don't blame anyone who wasn't there for not believing it happened. But I was there... and I know it happened."

"I didn't 'see it happen,' Captain, but I know for a fact y'all didn't just walk into that ballroom through the front door. I also know for a fact that you *were* in that auditorium, five klicks away, and didn't just walk from there–and Ruhl confirms that one as well."

"So we both keep having the same problem, General, as well as the same answer. Ruhl Skattersmythe and Saul Ellsberg both keep telling us fantastic things, *doing* fantastic things... and both keep corroborating each other. And it looks like it just happened again."

"Only *this* time," Bush said, "we ain't just talkin' about your pet writer and my pet alien tellin' the same stories. Mr. Ellsberg pulled his little trick on camera this time... and apparently arranged for some other evidence as well."

"It's all verified, then?" I asked.

"I'm not gonna get ahead of Sandy Lochardt's report, Captain, but the short answer is 'yes.' Everything you told our forensics lab to look for on that 'publication' checks out. What's more, *no one* at the Downtown Dallas Post Office has any recollection of havin' received it. It's like it materialized in that sortin' bin outta thin air."

"Which is *exactly* what Sr. Ellsberg claims happened. What about the map coordinates?"

"Again, you can get Sandy's report with the rest of us–but, yeah: DPS field agents have found witnesses at each one of those locations who confirm having seen someone who matches that 'person of interest' profile. We even have a confirmed border crossing at Rio Grande City."

He passed me a photostat of what looked like a Pacific Federation passport. "Miguel Estefan Alejandro Murphy?" I asked. The face on the photo looked young and possibly Asian. But also–possibly–*something else*, I thought, remembering Ruhl's Skattersmythe's beautiful, ruined features.

"That's the name on the passport," Bush replied. "But we got no record of him entering Texas on *any* passport. Also, the descriptions Sandy's field agents got from eye witnesses don't all sound exactly like the same guy. He may or may not be some kinda 'spaceman'... but this Mr. Murphy *does* not add up."

"But apparently he exists," I said. "And apparently really did travel cross country from Oregon to Guatemala."

"We still don't have confirmation on that last part," Bush said. "But it sure looks that way."

"Which gets us to the last part of the story," I replied.

"And gets us to the point where my own credibility finally stretches to the snapping point," Bush said. "This 'angels and demiurges' stuff is just too damned much, Captain–it's gonna take more than Ruhl & Mr. Ellsberg backin' each other up for me to buy *that*."

"I had similar reservations," I said. "And I still do. The funny thing is... my own research halfway validates that as well."

"*Really*, Captain Cullen?" Bush's face fell into its characteristic smirk. "I had no idea your career was so extensive."

"Part of the reason Admiral Díaz brought me into BSI was to analyze what appeared to be 'mystery disk' and 'ghost airship' reports going back over centuries," I said. "I teach history at the RCN Academy... so it's not as far a stretch as you might think.

"The interesting thing is that the reports stand up to historical analysis, if you're willing to approach them objectively. They also almost completely disappear from roughly 1500 to 1900 AD."

"And you think," Bush said, "this 'demiurgos' that Ruhl keeps goin' on about is the reason why?"

"Fortunately for us both, General, accepting this hypothesis costs neither Texas or California anything more than a can of paint–I'm good for it.

"How about *you*?"

# Part 4: The Crossroad and The Crucible

## *one: kayce*

Of course, Bush's 'ranch' had a bar.

I'd known about it for a few days, had not been inclined to check it out. But it had been a long day, ending with a difficult meeting. I felt like I could afford the indulgence.

On the bartender's advice, I had ordered something described as a 'habanero mango margarita on the rocks.' It would've been better with more habanero and less mango… but I've had worse.

While I was debating whether or not my self-indulgence extended to a second one, a voice said, "Mind if I join you?"

"I'd be honored, Agent Lochardt. Please have a seat."

Lindsay Lochart was a tall woman with iron-gray hair who typically favored corduroy blazers and dark shirts over the ubiquitous Texican dungarees and vaquero boots. Other than the fact that her role in Texas DPS wasn't too unlike my role in California BSI, I didn't really know much about her.

The bartender tried to interest her in one of the margaritas I was drinking. She opted instead for a Mexican lager. I decided to follow her example if I wound up staying for another round.

"So, what did you think about that briefing?" she asked. "No specifics, not sitting at a bar," she added. "In general."

"In general? In general. I'd say your team has done a fairly impressive job of validating something I still have a hard time believing. Good work on that."

"Thanks, Captain. You ain't the only one who has a hard time swallowin' all this. After I got cleared on 'Ghost One,' I figured I'd seen it *all*... obviously, I was wrong."

* * * *

The image on the screen was deceptively crude.

Printed in black and white on what looked like standard office copier printer paper, the title at the top read 'DEMIURGE, ARCHANGELS & ALIENS.' Beneath it, in smaller text but the same crude font: 'The HIDDEN CONSPIRACY of the Greater Cosmos.' Beneath that, an equally crude illustration of a pyramid rising from a jungle, an eye superimposed onto the pyramid's apex.

"Lab analysis confirms, to a high probability, that this 'publication' was produced via the same process as the two previous publications analyzed at BSI headquarters in California. Next slide, please."

The image changed; Agent Lochart continued. "We still have no idea how these materials are making their way into the downtown Dallas Post Office. For now, Mr. Ellsberg's explanation makes as much–or as little–sense as anything else we know."

"It's not *my* explanation," Saul said. "But it's as much as we are going to get. The clock's running, guys–can we get on with this?"

"We ain't got the inside scoop on this that you do, Mr. Ellsberg," General Bush said. "How about you just chill out and work with us on this?"

Saul shrugged. "Sure."

"Thanks, Lindsay," Bush said. "So, let's just assume that this is all legit. Why not? In case y'all ain't noticed, a lot of things are kinda crazy these days. What I need to know from the experts on my team is if there is any risk or liability to goin' through with this. Lindsay, you got the floor–I'm gonna start with you."

"Thanks, G.W." Agent Lochardt pointed to the screen. "My folks have confirmed that there is nothing *dangerous* about this paint formula. They've also confirmed that we can get the materials from pretty much any chemical supply house. We could get a batch of this stuff on a day's notice... if we're gonna do this."

"We're about to figure that one out," Bush said. "T.J.–what about you?"

"As near as I can tell," Major Kuehng replied, "all you need from my folks is a few Rangers to stand guard on a warehouse and another try at sendin' a drone into Guatemala. I got no problem with either–although I expect the drone'll just get shot down again."

"Not this time," Saul said. "You now have clearance."

"Clearance from *who*?" Kuehng asked. "The Central American government don't know *shit* about this operation–and I don't wanna hear nothin' about no 'archangel.'"

"Too bad," Saul said. "Because that's where your clearance came from."

"Thanks, T.J.," Bush said. "Charley, you're next. I'd also appreciate hearing from Dr. Albion." he turned to me. "If that's okay with you, Captain."

I shrugged. "This is a joint task force, and time is apparently something of a concern. That's fine by me."

* * * *

The Mexican lager was *definitely* an improvement.

"So I guess we're goin' ahead," Lindsay said.

"Seems that way," I replied. "At least for now."

"So... what's it like?"

"What is *what* like?"

"You know," she said. "The thing your writer buddy does."

"Oh, *that*. It's hard to describe. It's like blinking, only it's the *world* blinking. You're one place, then you're someplace else. But it's *really* hard to deal with. I can only clearly remember the last time it happened. The rest is a blur."

She took a swig from her lager. "I think I'll pass, thanks."

"Not high on my list of repeat experiences," I said. "Thanks, by the way."

"Thanks for what?"

"Asking me about it," I said. "Everyone seems to think I consider this normal, that I'm okay with it... I'm *not*. I really appreciate being able to talk about it–even though we can't *really* talk."

"Nope," Lindsay said. "Not here. Even though this place gets swept pretty regular for bugs, I can't rule out the possibility of someone here not bein' exactly what they seem to be–except for Sanchez." She pointed to the bartender, a dark-haired man of middle years with a large and expressive mustache. "Former Texas Devil; used to serve with T.J. & G.W. He is *exactly* what he seems."

"Does *everyone* here go by their initials?" I asked.

"It's a 'good ol' boy' thing," she replied. "I guess you ain't got them in California."

"You might be surprised," I told her.

* * * *

The screen had switched from showing photostats of *Demiurge, Archangels, and Aliens* to a video conference feed from Aurora, Texas. Ameryst Albion and Charley Hardin sat next to each other in what looked like the agriculture station office the Texicans had built over the wreckage of a 'Ghost Airship'.

Sitting fairly close to each other, it seemed... Interesting.

Ameryst had escaped with us when we left *Los Estados* two steps ahead of an autogyro attack group. She'd been a senior researcher in a program to decode another piece of crashed alien hardware, had been all too happy to leave once she knew her work was being hijacked to serve the current Yanquis *Presidente's* delusions.

Charley Hardin, I barely knew. He was an engineer on loan to the Texas Air Force from Hughes Aeronautics, had been bright enough to figure out that the wreckage of 'Ghost One' was trying to repair itself. Even more impressively, he'd figured out that the remains of the pilot weren't really dead... and could be repaired as well.

No doubt that Ameryst and Charley had a lot to talk about–when they weren't talking to the half-mechanical alien Charley had helped to restore. Young, bright people who had made a study of damaged things most people didn't even believe were real. They could spend the rest of their lives studying what Saul was offering to deliver.

Charley was tall and gangly, with brown skin and bleached, curly hair cropped short. Ametyst was short and stocky, red-haired and pale. She had the same nervous smile she'd had since the first day I'd met her, fidgeting with a lock of her own curly hair.

"Glad y'all could join us," General Bush said. "Had a chance to review that... comic book, or whatever you call it?"

"Fan pub," Ametyst said. "Short for 'fan publication.' A lot of people in the Sci-Rom community write them... just not like *this*."

"You got that *right*, Dr. Albion," Bush replied. "Charley, what's your take on this thing?"

"Most of this is really not my field, General," Charley said. "I've shown Ameryst the photography from when Ghost One was first recovered. Even though the materials are completely different, we're in agreement that both The Device warehoused at Dayton Aerodrome and Ghost One were damaged by exceptionally powerful lightning discharges.

"*Could* that discharge have been directed by an entity of some sort? Ghost One says that's what happened, and this 'fan pub' says the same thing–even if it doesn't say *how*. All this stuff about 'telekinesis' and 'teleportation' is just magic mumbo-jumbo masquerading as science, except for one thing: we *know* it's happening... even if we don't know *how*."

* * * *

"Another lager, Captain?"

"Thanks, Sanchez," I said. "But I don't think so–I have a busy day tomorrow."

"What about you, Lindsay?"

"Same–close me out as well." Agent Lochart drained her lager and turned to me with a crooked grin. "Gonna go see the tin man, are you? You know he's nuts, right?"

"So I've been told," I replied. "Unfortunately, he's also the only first-hand information source we have."

"Except for your Mr. Ellsberg,"

I shook my head. "Not even *Saul* considers himself a 'primary source', and I wouldn't want to solely rely on him, even if he were. The more connected to these things he becomes, the more erratic he is. I don't think he's 'nuts'–but I need as much information as I can before I'm comfortable making my next report to the RCN Admiralty."

"You can't just get Charley and Ameryst to talk to him for you?"

I shook my head again. “He’s an engineer, she’s a scientist. The things I need are the things they are least qualified to ask about. And, anyway, I don’t need to be here for the prep work going on in ‘Hanger 52.’ I can take the time.”

“Sure you don’t want me to tag along? I got the clearance.”

I smiled. “Thanks, Lindsay, but I’ll manage. The escort Major Kuehng’s providing is *more* than enough security. And I need some head space. I haven’t really had that for a while.

“Thanks for talking to me, though. I really appreciate that.”

She smiled back. “Any time… Kayce.”

### *two: murphy*

“You must *really* have a thing for Space Elfs, dude.”

“Apparently, it’s mutual,” I said. “And not anything I particularly expected.”

“*Really*?” Case said. “Then why’d you switch off ‘social interface’ before taking the call?”

I hadn’t even known what the call was when I took it, but I didn’t exactly feel like explaining that to my uninvited digital sidekick. If Case planned to continue ‘living’ in my head, he was just going to have to get used to playing by my rules.

“You’re either a ‘bug’ or an ‘undocumented feature,’ and the nearest support tech for this shit’s in a nearby alternate universe. I can’t take a chance on this hardware failing when I need it the most.”

“Fair,” he said.

When Aelia ended our virtual reality booty call, I returned to the reality of being in a cell in a repurposed Mayan temple, waiting for a crazy army dude to give me a choice between giving him insanely powerful objects I was expected to guard with my life or watching his troops start picking off hostages–starting with Aelia herself.

Aelia's consort, the immortal and semi-divine Astarte, was not likely to take that well. How she was going to feel about Aelia's dalliance with me was an interesting question, but I did not feel particularly threatened. I somehow doubted that a being as old as the universe itself was going to be the jealous type.

In any case, Astarte and I had a plan for dealing with Colonel Wolfreich and his occupation force–a plan it was time for me to start putting into motion.

Ever since he'd helped me get free of the psychic torture illusion Wolfreich's Grey had used to 'interrogate' me, Ghost Case had standardized on a single 'look'–an illusion of how his creator, Case Prime, had looked when we'd both been young: a cornfed kid from the Midwest, rocking a bad mullet and clothing straight out of *Miami Vice*.

The illusion was leaning against the wall of my cell, next to the makeshift 'door' that had replaced the one Wolfreich's troops had vaporized when they'd arrived. I didn't owe him much, but I least owed it to myself to be honest with him.

"We haven't really talked about it," I said. "But you realize there's a pretty non-zero chance I may not get clear of this in one piece."

"No need to talk about something *that* obvious," replied the ghost. "Unless *you* need to."

"Maybe I do, Case. I've been thinking a lot about what I *really* want to do. The problem with this whole 'rejuvenation' thing is that it's just *hardware*.

"Yeah, sure–the *body* got turned back into a young man with an interesting side-order of alien DNA. But what's *inside* that body is still an old man–an old man who has experienced *hundreds* of virtual lifetimes as a form of torture. Waking up knowing those lifetimes weren't real doesn't take away the trauma... or make me feel any less old."

"Are you saying you want to die?" Case asked.

"Not really," I replied. "But I'm having a hard time figuring out what to do with my life. I'm still more or less human. Going through the motions of being young again just ain't cutting it. If I have to make a judgment call between my own survival and something more important... I think I'm ready to make that call. Apologies in advance if you get cut off in the process."

He was completely still for a long moment, then glitched momentarily into static. It had been happening on the trip down here and was now happening more frequently. But Case didn't seem to know it was happening, and I had no idea what it meant.

Then he unfroze. "Apology accepted... I guess. I've been thinking a lot as well–I guess what I do is 'thinking.'

"I don't think I'm a full copy of Real Me. I remember the stuff you and he did decades ago like it was yesterday. I remember Real Me waking up to what we are. I remember Real Me torturing you. I remember *everything* that happened to him after that.

"But the *really* recent stuff, from just before Real Me made Fake Me? I think there's stuff missing. As much as I hate to admit it, I think I'm a 'curated' copy. I think he made me for a reason. I think there's a good chance that whatever you wind up doing *is* that reason.

"So, don't worry too much about apologizing to *me*, 'old buddy.' It's just as likely that the fucking Space Elfs made *you* for a reason as well. You could be just as much a 'fake' as I am–and there is *no way* you haven't thought about it... whether you want to admit it or not. As far as I know, everything you *think* you remember is true–but I'm hardly a 'reliable narrator'... am I?

"But even if this all ends badly, at least it *ends*.

"And I'm kinda okay with that."

### *three: kayce*

The courier bike I'd pulled from the motor pool was built for speed, the road I was on... not quite as much. As long as I stayed focused, I could keep up a good pace. Fortunately, there wasn't much other traffic. On the open stretches, I could open the throttle all the way.

When I'd asked General Bush if there was a quicker way to get to Aurora than the elaborate vehicle switch route through Fort Worth, he smirked his usual smirk and said, "Maybe, Captain... you ride?"

Yeah... I ride.

I'd sort of given it up when I got together with Esmerelda. She seemed to think anyone who liked motorcycles was beneath our social standing. It had been easier to go along with it than argue. A lot of things are like that when you get married.

But it's like they say: riding a bike is one of those things you don't forget. Lucky for me, there was a pro shop next to the motor pool where I could get little essentials like bike pants, boots, and gloves to pick up where my flight jacket left off–not to mention a decent helmet.

In my left rear-view mirror, I could see the occasional glint from a hard to see object above and behind me–my 'escort'. The remote controlled miniature airship was little different from the ones Major Kuehng and his team kept trying to send into Guatemala, except for one thing: this one was armed. It wouldn't be much help if I lost control and wound up in a ditch, but anyone who tried to impede my progress was going to be in for a rude awakening.

Bush was right. Between the lack of traffic and a shorter route, I would be arriving at the 'agricultural station' outside Aurora at least an hour more quickly than the last time, maybe less if I *really* pushed it. Depending on how much time I spent talking to Ruhl, I would likely be back at Hughes Aerodrome by sundown.

After an hour on the road, I fell into *exactly* the mental state I'd been hoping for. The part of me that wasn't pushing a motorcycle as hard as I could was free to reflect. The world had gone slightly crazy in the last year, gotten slightly more crazy in the last month, and–at least for me–changed *completely* in the last week.

If this latest promised impossibility turned out to be true, *someone's* world was going to get even crazier... but that someone wouldn't be me. I could go back to playing chess and occasionally fencing with my pops, donning dress whites and going to the opera with my wife–hell, just *being* with my wife.

No one was going to ask me to run the 'Bureau of Exotic Technology Analysis' the Admiralty was putting together. More likely than not, that would wind up being Hiram Díaz's responsibility. I could *finally* go back to teaching history at the academy.

I had *maybe* exaggerated my need to have another in-person conversation with Ruhl Skattersmith to justify this trip... but only a little. Even though the resources we were putting at Saul Ellsberg's disposal were slight, they needed to be justified. And if a half dead 'aethernaut' was going to tell me that roughly half of what I thought I knew about history was wrong... I needed specifics. I needed more than fantastic 'fan publications' and Saul Ellsberg teleporting himself out of an isolation tank.

I needed the *truth*–assuming an actual 'truth' was out there.

* * * *

Mariella had escorted me into the back office of 'Texas Agricultural Extension Service, Station 22', insisting that I stay for a brief lunch before heading back to San Antonio. I agreed, as long as she could be quick about it–I was determined to be back in San Antonio before sunset. She opened the disguised entrance for me, and I descended into the hidden space that had once been an abandoned mine.

I couldn't be sure, but it seemed to me that the crashed 'ghost airship' the Texicans had code-named 'Ghost One' was even more close to repairing itself than the last time I had seen it, mere days ago. The hull was still pierced where it had been struck by lightning, but the discoloration was fading, and the hole looked smaller. I wondered for a moment how the Texicans planned to get it out, if it ever became *fully* operational.

Most likely, they hadn't planned that far in the first place.

I knocked, then entered the dark and cluttered space of Ruhl's 'workshop.' The cinnamon-like scent was even more pungent than the last time, even though the underlying odor of decay seemed less. Fresh from my ride, I noticed how cool the space was. The Texicans had to be spending a small fortune on air conditioning–but, given that underlying smell of decay... maybe they *had* to.

I seated myself at the near end of the work table, just as cluttered with books, magazines, and disassembled machines as the list time I'd seen. Prominent in the clutter was a photostat copy of *Demiurge, Archangels, and Aliens*. We'd debated whether or not to show it to him at all, but he'd already confirmed half of it before we'd even received it. Half of the rest he'd know about anyway, if the proposed plan actually worked.

It was the remaining half I needed to ask him about.

Ruhl Skattersmythe entered from what I assumed must be some sort of bed chamber deeper in the darkness. Did he even sleep? I wondered. Or had being 'dead' for the better part of a century been as much sleep as his kind even needed?

Inhumanly tall, inhumanly thin, his slanting eyes and high cheekbones reminded me of the man I'd seen in a copied passport photo–although that man was apparently otherwise human.

"Hello, Captain Cullen," Ruhl said, as he took the seat across the table from me. "Mariella told me you would be coming. From what I understand, I should be congratulating you for now being a 'captain.' Is it your intention to one day become an 'admiral' like Díaz or a 'general' like Bush?"

"No," I said. "It is not."

"I was curious," he said. "I know that such things are of importance to your people. How can I help you?"

Even seated, he towered over me. A long, loose black robe concealed most of his body, except for a skeletally lean arm, encased in assorted wires and cables, some of which seemed to enter into his flesh. The same wires and cables traced along his neck and framed his face, before disappearing into the long, iron-gray hair bound behind his head.

His visible skin color still varied from corpse gray to raw pink to a coppery bronze hue, but it seemed that the gray was fading. The blue eyes seemed even more piercingly aware. I could understand why General Bush said that Ruhl occasionally frightened him.

"We need to talk about this," I said, picking up the staple-bound photostat.

"I have discussed it already with Charley Hardin and his new friend, Doctor Albion. They asked many questions." He inclined one slanted eyebrow with a look of indifferent amusement. "Questions I could not answer for them are questions I cannot answer for you."

"I understand that," I said. "But Charley Hardin is an engineer and Dr. Albion is a scientist. I accept their judgment on the things they are qualified to ask you. But I was a historian before I joined the California Navy. I have qualifications they lack.

"When I met you, you told me things about my world's history that contradict much of what I know. This publication makes similar claims. We need to talk about that."

"Most of this I understand," he replied. "Although some of it is almost meaningless. The distinctions your people make among yourselves are not the distinctions my people make. But I will tell you what I can."

"I appreciate that," I told him. "There's just one other thing, and I can't *believe* no one else has bothered to ask. We're about to steal a spaceship. If it's what we think it is, there's a good chance you could steal it from *us*.

"*Are you?*"

* * * *

There was even less traffic on the road for my return trip, enabling me to run the courier bike as fast as it would go. The lowering sun to my right was nicely offset by the waxing moon rising to my left. Anything not in my headlights was illuminated brightly enough to be easily avoided. I once had to veer hard to the left to avoid an armadillo trying to cross the road, but that was the only interruption to the steady passage of miles.

At least at first.

My aerial escort from *Los Diablos de Tejanos* was hard to see in the waning light, but I knew it was still there. I knew I would safely make my way back to San Antonio, where decisions waited for me that I had put off long enough.

Backing Ruhl into a corner where he could not evade questions had been fairly simple once I had him in a one-on-one conversation. I still wasn't sure all the answers I'd gotten were the complete and unvarnished truth, but I was fairly certain *Ruhl* understood the limits on his credibility and my credulity.

It wasn't all that different from explaining to my students what they could and could not get away with on an exam or a term paper. Once they understand that the easy lies aren't going to fly, they either start doing the work or start fabricating more complicated lies. On the other hand, Ruhl Skattersmythe was orders of magnitude smarter than a first-year naval cadet.

He was also orders of magnitude more shameless. Maybe he really *was* at least five hundred years old. It was like General Bush had said: every once in a while, the affable mask slipped just enough. Just enough to see what Ruhl's kind thought of humankind. Just enough to see how little he cared to owe his restored life to us. Just enough to wonder if he considered what Charley Hardin had done for him to be 'life' at all.

In any case, he'd told me what I needed to know, including the parts where he claimed to know little more than I did. There weren't *many* of those... but at least he was admitting them.

* * * *

"Really? You've been at war for a few *thousand* years?"

"I am uncertain that 'war' is exactly the right word," Ruhl replied. "But more than a *few* thousand years. The little grey people and my folk have been in conflict since before your own kind had language or the use of fire.

"My own kind had advanced further than yours when the little grey people began to prey upon us–although what they did was much the same. There was no *demiurgos* stranded on our Earth, no self-appointed 'protector' to strike down invaders from elsewhere. But we did not need one. Unlike you... we could defend ourselves."

"According to this," I pointed again to *Demiurge, Archangels, and Aliens*, "that conflict has played out on more than a few worlds. What, exactly, is 'The Greater Cosmos'? A multiverse?"

"It is what my people found when we tried to find our way to the stars," Ruhl said. "*Not* 'the multiverse,' for that is chaos–the totality of all that has ever been, is, or could be. Neither your kind nor mine could function in *that*." He shuddered. "As to the Greater Cosmos: there are places where space is thin and universes connect–but only across millions of years of crosstime... at least, it would seem, until now."

"Do you know why this has changed?"

"I do not. I only know what I see."

"Let's get back to immediate specifics," I said. "Saul Ellsberg is claiming to be in contact with a half-human being who made the original copy of this publication appear in a location about 80 kilometers east of here.

"This half-human says he can deliver a 'ghost airship'–the same one *you've* been tracking–if we just follow the instructions in this pamphlet. We have eyewitness testimony from places where you've tracked this thing. Minus the hole in the side, it sounds just like your ship. Assuming all this is any less crazy than it sounds, and we wind up with this thing, why would you not just take it from us... and go home?"

He smiled sadly, then the smile and the arrogance both went away... leaving only the sadness. "There is a reason why I cannot do this, and a reason why I *would not* do this. And they are the same." He held up his cable encrusted, mottled arm. As he did, the robe fell away, revealing even more of it. He pointed to the cables with the skeletally thin forefinger of his other hand.

"This," he said, "was not always a *part* of me. When I came here, all of this lay over my skin. My species evolved on an 'Earth,' but my people have adapted to another world with lower gravity. You would call it 'Mars,' even though it is not *your* Mars. Without the support of an exoskeleton, I could neither stand nor walk on your world.

"When the *demiurgos* struck me down, the only reason I did not truly die was because my exoskeleton took extreme measures to preserve me. By the time your people found and restored me... those measures became permanent. My exoskeleton is a part of my ship and is now part of me. I cannot do as you suggest."

"You also said you *would* not," I replied. "May I ask why?"

"That is less easily explained, Captain Cullen... but I will try. My people call ourselves 'The Fortuned.' We are proud; we are vain. We consider ourselves beautiful. None among my kind would see beauty in what I have become. They would see only shame."

"Even though 'what you have become' occurred in their service?"

He shook his head. "It would make no difference."

* * * *

I hadn't gotten all the answers I'd wanted, but I'd gotten enough.

With the sun fully down, my drone escort was now completely invisible. But I knew it was there, even though I was more doubtful than ever that I really needed it. The Yanquis had either been bluffing all along or had been entirely deceived by their new 'allies.' Either way, they weren't going to be sending anything into Texas airspace any time soon.

Soon enough, I wouldn't need it, anyway. I was back in San Antonio, Hughes Aerodrome was now minutes away. The promised lunch back in Aurora had taken longer than I'd wanted... but it had been worth it.

Even though the traffic was picking up, I kept the throttle on the bike wide open. I'd forgotten how much I missed this. Hopefully, Esmerelda would be happy enough to have me back to forgive a few returned old habits.

With any luck, I'd get back in time to grab a snack and a beer at Sanchez's bar–maybe a couple of beers, if Agent Lochardt happened to turn up.

I found myself thinking about poor, ruined Ruhl Skattersmythe. I no longer doubted that his people had once ruled mine, even though I had doubts about a demiurgic 'fallen angel' with the power to rewrite history. But just enough of what he said aligned with just enough of my own research into the history of 'mystery disks' and 'ghost airships'. I could no longer discount *any* of it out of hand.

I still had some profound doubts about the 'technology' of what Saul and his supposed half-alien contact were proposing–but, thankfully, no one was asking me to validate *that*.

* * * *

"Except for the high probability of looking stupid, no real risk I can see. More tortillas, Captain?"

"Thanks, but no thanks–I need to hit the road."

Marietta Cohen's promised 'brief lunch' turned out to include a fairly substantial posole and a side dish of assorted braised greens from her personal garden plot. Finding out that Marietta was yet another combat-trained member of DPS Special Ops surprised me not at all. Finding out that she was an outstanding cook as well probably shouldn't have surprised me either.

But it did.

I passed the plate of tortillas to Charley Hardin, who smiled as he took a couple and held the plate for Ameryst Albion–who smiled back and briefly shook her head. The impression I'd had, that something *other* than mutual curiosity about alien technology was going on between them, had solidified not long after I arrived.

No surprise, really. They were both young and reasonably attractive. If the admiralty expected me to enforce the terms of Ameryst's asylum application, they might have to settle for my resignation. Although, if this 'plan' worked... there would be more than sufficient reason to keep her here.

"On a 'cost to risk' analysis," Charley said, handing the tortillas back to Marietta. "This is a *way* better deal than bringing back Ruhl was in the first place... *if* it works."

"And what are your thoughts on that?" I asked.

"This is more Ameryst's field than mine," Charley replied. "All I *really* know about this 'teleportation' stuff is that it's supposed to be something these Grey Aliens do. Ruhl's confirmed that–but he doesn't have any more idea how it works than we do."

"Ruhl might know more than he's saying," Ametyst chimed in. "Now that I've had a chance to look at 'Ghost One,' I think there's a high probability that Ruhl's people did what we've been trying to do: reverse engineer working principles from a crashed Grey ship. But where we failed... they succeeded."

"It would explain a lot," I said, thinking about the plot of one of my pops' sci-rom books.

Ametyst nodded. "I'm pretty sure that *all* of these different crosstime species have tech using the same principles, even if their engineering is completely different. But I'm not completely sure that teleportation, or whatever we want to call it, even qualifies as *technology*. It's more like magic or biology... or some weird mix of the two."

"Sufficiently advanced technology is indistinguishable from magic," Charlie intoned.

"So my pops always said," I replied. "But I'm beginning to think the reverse is true as well."

"I guess we're about to find out," Marietta said. "More posole?"

### *four: murphy*

Of course, Wolfreich cheated on the deadline... just like I knew he would.

The door crashing open in the early morning hours was as predictable as the helmet-mounted lamps glaring into my eyes. If the guns, body armor, and face-covering visors were supposed to frighten or intimidate, they were in for a bit of a disappointment.

I was dressed for them and waiting, had been for hours. Instead of the linen shirt and pants I'd been wearing since my arrival, I'd switched back to the dungarees and leather I'd worn on the road down from Oregon.

'Social interface' was switched off. Ghost Case had done everything he could. He'd either be a distraction or a liability at this point. It felt strangely lonely, not having him in my head. But unlike most of the people, real or imagined, who had ever disappeared from my life... at least I'd had a chance to say goodbye.

See you on the other side, Case.

"Get to your feet. Keep your hands where I can see them," said a voice I remembered. I wondered how his nose was doing under the visor. Probably not all that great.

"The colonel will see you *now*," he said, gesturing toward the door with his weapon.

It was a short trip from my cell to the temple dais at the top of the pyramid. I could see a brightening to the east, where the sun would soon rise. At the end of the dais, Colonel Wolfreich stood.

Except for the helmet, he was in the same battle dress as his men: tactical black greaves, vambraces, and body armor over black fatigues, a holstered sidearm on his right hip. Unlike the stolen alien weapons his men carried, the sidearm looked like an automatic pistol, hardly any different from the ones I used to carry.

The battle dress fatigues also looked like something I might've worn, once upon a time, except for the American flag patch on the shoulder. I'd always been a 'plausibly deniable' asset, whether I was doing The Company's dirty work or The Order's.

And even if I'd ever worn such a thing, it would've only had 50 stars on it. But no one had ever had to make America 'great' again, where Wolfreich was from–it had been a racist empire all along.

My escort prodded me to one side of the dais as Astarte and Aelia arrived, prodded to the other side by two more armed guards. They were wearing the same linen gowns they had worn when I first met them–minus their jewelry, which I assumed the soldiers had stolen.

Turning, Wolfreich pointed to the mottled golden serpent draped about 'Astarte's' neck. His gray eyes narrowed in contempt as his scarred lip wrinkled under his mustache. "Why," he asked, "did you bring *that* thing?"

"Sorry, sir," said the escort. "It's not a *real* snake. It's like it's welded to her skin or something. We couldn't remove it."

"More Barsoomian decadence, I suppose," he said in his not-quite southern drawl. "Doesn't much matter." He turned to me. "My orders were to take this man from his bed. Why is he dressed like that?"

"That's how we found him," said my escort. "It's like he was waiting for us."

"I cain't say I'm surprised," Wolfreich said, as he crossed over to where I stood. "You look like a man dressed for a fight, Mr. Murphy. You aimin' to be a problem for us?"

"Last time I checked," I said, "you were the ones with the guns."

"Indeed we are, sir. And this is about as good a place as any to us 'em. You've had your three days, more or less. It's time we resume our little chat." He looked past my shoulder to one of the men standing behind me. "Fetch the wog."

"I thought we'd already figured out that doesn't work on me," I said.

"Oh, we did," Wolfreich replied. "But they have their *other* uses." He looked past my shoulder again. "Bring out our other guest, please."

### *five: kayce*

"Sure you don't want a hot dog? They're really good."

"Only if you have one that's vegan," I replied.

Saul laughed, then snorted. "In *Texas*? Yeah, right."

"How are you managing to do this without setting off the fire alarm?" I asked.

"Major Kuehng disconnected it. As long as he and his guys get some as well. It's cool."

It didn't sound very 'cool' to me, but as Saul had pointed out... we were in Texas. He'd made good use of his time while I'd been on the road. As my eyes adjusted to the gloom in the hangar, I could see everything that the thing had instructed us to do.

There were lines drawn on the concrete floor in silvery paint, forming an irregular hexagram with one axis almost twice as long as the other two. The vertices of the long axis were capped with circles, roughly 12 meters across.

The circle at the far vertex held the tank Charley Hardin had used to resurrect Ruhl Skattersmythe and later used to force Saul into an altered state of consciousness... an altered state that was beginning to seem permanent. I couldn't be sure, but it looked like additional equipment had been added to the top and the base.

The circle at the near vertex, the one I was standing in, contained a larger assortment of a somewhat different nature: a construction site portable toilet, a portable folding table, an ice chest, a small charcoal grill, and a portable camp chair. Taped to the side of the toilet: a hand-lettered sign that read 'HANGAR 52.' Sitting on the table: a typewriter and several notebooks. Sitting on the grill: a number of small sausages. Sitting in the chair: Saul Ellsberg.

He'd shed more than his tweed jacket in response to the heat. He was wearing what looked like gym shoes and shorts, with a mostly unbuttoned Hawai'ian shirt. I couldn't blame him. Even with an industrial grade warehouse fan positioned at either end of the warehouse, the hanger felt like an oven.

"I'm sorry it's so crowded in here," he said, blinking behind his tinted glasses. "I guess I could've made the circles bigger. You don't need to be in the circle, you know… just me."

"How long do you need to be here?" I asked.

He shrugged. "I don't know. Until the thing happens. You know: *the thing*." Even though he was speaking in a flat monotone, his eyes were wide. I decided he was right… I *didn't* need to be standing in the circle.

"Have you talked to Helene about this?"

"About what? The circles? The hotdogs?"

"*Any* of it," I said.

"He has," said Helene Abenard's voice from behind me. "Saul, do you mind terribly if Kayce and I go somewhere to talk? The smoke is burning my eyes."

Saul waved his hand. "Sure, no problem. Hey, on the way out, can you tell the guys their dogs are ready?"

* * * *

"One iced herbal tea, Doc," Sanchez said. "Sure you don't want a shot with it?"

Helene smiled. "I'm fine. Thank you, Sr. Sanchez."

As Sanchez walked away, I sipped on a sweetened iced tea of my own. We'd gotten a booth in the back of Sanchez's bar, which I'd expected to be fairly empty this time of day. I was right. As usual, the air conditioning was running just above meat locker temperature. Thinking of Saul, I felt a little guilty… but only a little.

“Are you certain this is a safe place to talk?” Helene asked me.

I smiled. “I am, actually. Sanchez is retired Special Ops and has this place swept regularly for bugs. I’d be careful what I say when it’s crowded, but right now it should be fine. In any case,” I took another sip of my tea, “who’d believe a single word they overheard?”

“Good point,” she replied. “Where shall we begin?”

“I was away for a single *day*, Helene. Has something been going on with Saul I hadn’t noticed?”

“Probably a lot, given your current responsibilities. But how reasonably can we *not* expect him to exhibit changes in behavior?

“We’re both guilty of the same oversight. You, Saul, and I have been through the same experiences. We’ve watched him change slowly over time, as the things happening to him change as well. And because he was changing in ways that made him seem more ‘normal,’ we accepted the changes without even thinking about it.”

“That’s true,” I said. “I have a hard time sometimes believing he’s the same man Admiral Díaz had me ‘arrest’ a year ago.”

“He’s *not*,” Helene replied. “All that man knew was that he was having dreams that weren’t really his–dreams of things that had actually happened that he couldn’t know about, dreams of things that wound up becoming real. But he didn’t know how, he didn’t know why.”

“Well… now we know.”

“*We* don’t know anything, Kayce. We know that *something* reaches out through him to do things that I still have difficulty convincing myself have truly happened. He now tells us that he knows what this ‘something’ is, *who* this something is. But what he tells us is even more bizarre than the things that keep happening *to him* that we also experience."

"So what do I do now, Helene? He's my *friend*, damn it. And my friend is sitting in an airship hangar, getting shithammered on cheap Mexican lager and grilling hot dogs for a squad of Texas Rangers. And what's with the typewriter? Is he actually *writing* anything?"

"Not so far," she replied. "He tells me that he's had no further dream conversations with this supposed half-alien he calls 'Colvin Case.' But he is also telling me that he's not dreaming anything else. For the first time in his current conscious memory, he effectively *has no dreams*."

"How is that even possible? *Everyone* has dreams."

"Not the way Saul does. Maybe he's just having normal dreams for the first time in his life... and doesn't know what they are. But everything he's done as a writer has been based on his dreams. Now he's trying to write without them."

"Do you know what he's writing?" I asked.

Helene shook her head. "He does not want to show it to anyone just yet. If it gives him something to do besides drink and grill sausages, it receives my approval as his therapist."

"Do you *really* think that a 'ghost airship' is going to magically appear in that diagram?"

"I only know that *Saul* thinks so. How long are you prepared to let this go on?"

I took another sip of disgustingly sweet tea. "That's a good question. General Bush says we can have the hanger as long as we want, even though he's not going to have a guard posted on it indefinitely. Admiral

Díaz has convinced the admiralty to give me discretion on this, at least for now.

"On the other hand, that shipyard john Saul's using as a toilet is going to need servicing at some point, or that hangar's going to smell worse than grilled hotdogs. If you have no pressing concerns for Saul's mental health, I'm willing to let this run for a while. But if he tries to talk the Rangers into making a beer run... I'm pulling the plug."

### *six: murphy*

Since I knew he wanted to have an audience, I knew Wolfreich would wait until the sun was fully up before making any more moves... and I was right.

He'd set the stage nicely. To the left of the temple dais sat the liquid-filled tube holding his 'moon wog'–the enslaved Grey Case had decided to call 'Celeste.' Next to the tube was a table full of equipment connected to the tube by a number of cables; behind the table a bored-looking technician in a gray jumpsuit.

To the right stood Astarte, Aelia, and Sister Guadalupe. Astarte seemed lost in thought, her black eyes staring into nothing. Only Aelia and I knew that the tall, black-haired woman was nothing more than a puppet. The true 'Astarte,' the burning ember of sentient primordial matter from the dawn of time, now dwelt in the seeming of a mottled serpent draped on the puppet's shoulders.

Next to her stood Aelia. Her magenta hair shining in the stark morning light, her blue eyes imperious and impassive, she was the most compelling sight I could imagine. Catching my eye, the faintest of smiles crossed her lips for a moment. She would do as she must... and so would I.

Lastly stood Sister Guadalupe, wearing the simple linen dress of La Comuna, cinched tightly with the same black belt and crescent scabbard I was wearing as well. She was either being punished for being my friend, or to be made an example of the cost of resistance–but only if I failed to lead Colonel Wolfreich what he *thought* I was concealing.

And that wasn't going to happen.

In the courtyard below us, I could see La Comuna gathered under the watchful eyes of perhaps half a dozen more of Wolfreich's heavily armored 'Space Force' troops. I wondered again just how many of them there really were. Was Wolfreich insane enough, desperate enough, or audacious enough to bluff his way into trying to conquer this world with a handful of troops and a cache of advanced stolen weapons? Or maybe he just wanted to go home. I know that feeling well enough.

Too bad he wasn't going to get either one.

After speaking briefly to the technician monitoring 'Celeste.' he walked over to me. Tall, and big the way I was when I was *really* young, I could see from his body language that he was used to getting as much as he could from intimidation. I could also guess from the scar his mustache didn't really conceal he didn't just rely on intimidation.

I could also guess, from the way he kept trying to impress me, that it *really* bothered him that I flat just didn't give a shit. As he got closer, I could smell the pomade in the gray buzz cut hair.

My god, what a vain prick.

"I think you probably know how this works, Mr. Murphy," Wolfreich said. "But I *do* prefer to make sure of things. Three hostages, three times I ask you the same question.

“The technician assures me that the wog does *not* have to be in your mind to tell whether or not *you* are telling the truth. Or you could make this *much* simpler... and just tell me what I need to know.”

“What about the part,” I said, “where I give you what you want... and you start executing motherfuckers anyhow, motherfucker?”

“Oh, I suppose I could give you my ‘word as a gentleman’–but I expect we both know what *that’s* worth. About as much as your sister wives’ lives, or that old woman. One way or another, you’re just playin’ for time, sir.

“Amon jutoosh, Dawn Matter, *whatever* you want to call it.

“Where is it?”

“There is a small mountain to the northwest of this place. About fifteen klicks that way,” I said, jerking my head in the correct direction. “Near the summit, there is a cave. What you are asking me to reveal is in that place.”

Wolfreich looked to the technician, who looked up from his console and nodded.

“One more thing you should know,” I said. It was time to find out if Case’s alleged deal with ‘Celeste’ was any goddam good or not. “You will not gain entry *or* open the vault unless Astarte, Aelia, and I are *all* there. The locks are keyed to our presence... and ours alone. We must *all* go there... together.”

Wolfreich looked at the technician again... who nodded again.

“It sounds like we have an accord, then,” Wolfreich said. He looked at the technician again. “Tell the watch officer I need the ship’s boat. And you can go ahead and pack up–we’re done here. Just one last thing, Mr. Murphy.”

“What’s that?”

He waved his hand in Sister Guadalupe’s direction. “Since you didn’t say anything about needin’ this old woman to open your vault, any particular reason why we should take her along?”

I had a bad feeling about where this was going, but there wasn’t much I could do about it. “No. You can just let her go.”

“Oh, I *could*... but I won’t.”

* * * *

The ‘ship’s boat’ turned out to be exactly what it sounded like. The same spindle shape as the ghost airship itself, only smaller and with an open cockpit with just enough room for Wolfreich, two of his goons, Astarte, Aelia, and me.

I didn’t realize Aelia had clasped my hand until she ‘spoke’ to me, from her implant to mine. The last look on Sister Guadalupe’s face was the only thing I could really see.

I felt nothing.

*There was nothing you could do*, said the cooly reserved voice in my audio implant.

*I could have said we needed her as well*, I replied in the same silent voice.

*He would not have believed it*, she said. *And might well have become suspicious had the Selenite confirmed it as well.*

And then another voice, Astarte’s. “*They will pay*,” she said.

*What’s one more life to you, either of you, who have seen so many?* I replied.

*Had I a soul,* Astarte replied, *it would have broken billions of years and trillions of lives before your world was ever made–broken over the injustice that God made you both mortal and aware. But even a fallen angel such as I has faith that God will redeem that injustice. And this injustice as well.*

*And yet,* I replied, *you will still find a way to make these murders pay?*

*I did mention that I was a fallen angel... did I not?*

*Time for this later,* Aelia interjected. *We have work to do.*

The 'small mountain' I had pointed out was now looming before us. It hadn't seemed particularly small when I'd pushed my old Canadian surplus bike up the side of it to stash it against my future needs. It had seemed bigger yet, decades ago, when I'd visited its counterpart on my own Earth.

I was already old then, too old to be doing such things. But I wanted to see as much of what Astarte's counterpart, Morningstar, had gifted me as I could. Like most of what he'd given me, it was a jumble of things I could sell to museums, things I could sell to jewelers, and things that were pretty much junk.

Astarte was apparently a bit more fastidious than Morningstar. Once I figured out that the trick for getting in was the same, I'd had no trouble finding room to stash the old motorcycle and my knapsack–the *real* knapsack I'd brought to this world, with its hidden stash of gemlike objects that would register from a distance as 'dawn matter.'

Wolfreich interrupted my reverie. "You gonna tell me where to set down, Mr. Murphy? Or do we need to start playin' guessin' games again?"

"There," I told him, pointing to a level clearing not far from the summit.

After the sun went down, the hangar got a lot more bearable.

Major Kuehng and his Rangers were better company than I'd expected. Kuehng had already warned me to watch what I was saying... so I did.

"All these boys know is that ain't nobody goin' in or out of that hangar without me or G.W. sayin' it's cool. All this *other* stuff–angels, aliens, whatever, just keep that on the downlow, okay??"

"Got it, Major," I replied. "So let's just say that some sort of alien spacecraft appears in this airship hangar, and it happens to have a few heavily armed Yanquis in it from another universe. Are your 'boys' gonna know what to do?"

"One hundred percent, Mr. Ellsberg," Kuehng said, taking a long swig off his Shiner Bock. "These fellers ain't been through as much shit as you have, but it is *far* from their first rodeo. You just get that thing here... we'll do the rest."

So, I cooked up hot dogs for a half-dozen heavily armed Texas Rangers who had exactly one beer each before going back outside to do the same thing I was doing: waiting for something no one believed was really going to happen.

Including, just maybe... me.

I could tell that I was losing credibility pretty damned fast–but I didn't know what to do about it. You'd think that providing proof that Case and his buddy Murphy actually existed would be *good enough*... but apparently not.

So, I'm sitting here in the dark, waiting for something to happen. And–to be honest–I'm a little scared. Getting the chip out of my brain? That's *great*. Even if I don't remember what it's like not to have one, the people who *don't* have one seem to be a lot happier than I am.

But what if Case snags a little bit more than just the chip? When he teleported me out of the tank, a lot of the fluid in the tank went with me. What happens if a little bit of my brain goes away when the chip does?

Case says not to worry, but I get the distinct impression this is *not* the first line of shit he's ever sold. The idea that he and I are both just waiting for some guy named Murphy to do–I don't know, *something*–is more than a little disturbing.

At least I'm not in that damned tank... but this isn't much better.

I opened another beer and thought about grilling more hot dogs. They were *way* better than the dogs I remember getting back in San Francisco. The beer in Texas sucked, but other things almost made up for it.

Trying to write earlier hadn't gotten very far. I was beginning to wonder if I *could* write, if I didn't have a chip in my head feeding me impossible dreams.

Just maybe, without the chip... I didn't need to.

It really, really *sucks* that I can't remember who I used to be. I made a life being a writer, because it's all I had. Then I made a life working for BSI, because the alternative was going to jail. I don't even *know* what my alternatives are now.

Maybe I don't have any.

Whatever that asshole Murphy is doing... he needs to do it *faster*.

I can't keep doing this.

## *eight: murphy*

*Follow my lead,* I said to my 'sisters.' *He does not know that the Selenite lies for us.*

*The Selenite that is no longer here,* replied Aelia. *No offense to my mother's people or you, but how much more of this creature's posturing must we endure?*

*Not much,* I replied.

From the clearing where Wolfreich had moored his 'ship's boat', it was a short walk down a clear path to the cave's entrance. Aelia and 'Astarte' walked behind me, behind them Wolfreich, behind him the two guards with the same stolen weapons that had vaporized poor Sister Guadalupe.

Either there was no 'safety setting' on these weapons, as I had hoped, or Wolfreich's 'wog' had already disabled it. In either case, I could not escape the sense that I had caused someone's death.

No matter how much you tell yourself you are used to it... you aren't.

In my long service to corrupt causes, there's been more than a few deaths. The ones I personally made happen bother me. But the ones that happened *because* of me bother me a lot, lot more.

I agreed with Astarte: one way or another... Wolfreich was going to pay.

At the entrance to the cave, I stopped and let Aelia and Astarte's puppet stand beside me. Any one of us could have opened it, but we needed Wolfreich to believe we were all required. As one, we put our hands on what looked like a solid rock face.

And it opened.

We entered. If Wolfreich and his men felt slighted that we did not defer to them and their stolen weapons... that was *their* problem.

Not far within the cave were the things I'd left there. To one side, the old surplus motorcycle I'd acquired and restored not long after I'd arrived in this world. To the other, my knapsack–my *real* knapsack–with the artfully concealed objects an enslaved Grey alien had mistakenly identified as 'dawn matter.'

"Is this it, Mr. Murphy?" Wolfreich said. "I'm not seeing anythin' that looks like a 'vault.' Unless you somehow figured out how to lie to my wog... I think we might be back to playin' guessin' games. You still get three guesses, of course."

I turned to face him. "Too fucking bad your 'wog' ain't here to play referee, you little shit. You use your goddam ray guns on *anybody* at this point, and you got exactly *nothing*."

*Is this close enough?* I subverbalized to Astarte. *Or do you need more?*

*I can see the things you brought,* she replied. *Not what you were told, exactly, but I can still use them. I need closer, I need more time.*

*This is about to get complicated,* I replied. *Aelia, accept my apologies if this fails.*

*None needed,* she said. *You are fit company to die with... should all else fail.*

"What you are looking for is in that knapsack," I said. "Go ahead; help yourself."

Wolfreich smiled. "I was born at night, Mr. Murphy, but it wasn't *last* night. Why don't you just fetch it for me?"

"I can do that," I said.

*I can buy you a minute, Astarte... no more. I suggest you both ease away to either side.*

It really wouldn't have made a difference either way–but I was okay with this.

I walked around where the bag sat on the floor. I knew it was going to be tight.

But I knew I could do it.

I knelt before the knapsack I'd fetched across two worlds and a thousand miles.

I looked at Aelia. I saw Evangeia, Caroline, and so many others–too many, really.

I looked at Astarte's contrived puppet, the artificed 'serpent' she'd become draped about the puppet's neck. I thought about what a rare, fine privilege it was to have become the friend and confidant of *angels*.

I looked at Wolfreich and his men, pointing their silly little stolen ray guns at me as though that made them any more than thieves, as though the stupid fucking flag on their arms made them anything other than murderers. I saw my own history of casual murder and violence... and knew I was no better.

Finally, I looked inside *myself*, as time slowed to a crawl. I knew I could do this thing. I knew that it *mattered*.

I said a few choice words in old High Lemurian as the bag fell open, only a few of which would translate into 'fuck you, asshole.'

The ‘fake service revolver’ leapt from the bag and into my hand. I’ll give Wolfreich credit for being fast. His side arm had almost lined up with my face when I shot his–no ‘non-lethal’ option for *him*.

I was debating my next target... when the white light consumed me.

Followed by *nothing*.

# Epilogue

### *one: kayce*

"This," said Agent Lochardt, "is Hightower Observation Aerostat." The image on the screen gave no sense of scale, but it looked big. A silver sphere tethered to a ring made of thin metal girders, bristling with equipment.

"It was originally commissioned," she continued, "in 2016, as part of a joint effort between Texas and Central America to control the flood of illegal guns and narcotics coming from the United States. It has some of the best optical and electrowave sensors available *anywhere*."

"Manufactured in California, *right*?" Saul Ellsberg said. We'd found him unconscious when the 'event' occurred, he'd stayed that way for several days. Once more in his familiar oxford shirt and chinos, he at least *looked* like the 'Saul Ellsberg' I knew.

"For the most part," she admitted. "Since it was already pointed in the right direction, more or less, we've been using it to monitor the coordinates you supplied us in Guatemala."

"Interesting that we're only hearing about this now," I said.

"It's our platform, Captain," General Bush said. "We can do whatever we want with it. Just because we're partners on the one thing don't mean we're partners on *everything*. Hell, I'll even do business with *yankees*–assumin' I can find one that ain't a damn liar."

The first official weekly meeting of the now official "exotic technologies" joint partnership was going about as well as could be expected. Fortunately, it would soon no longer be my problem.

“Apologies, Captain Cullen,” Agent Lochart said. “Let’s not forget that, a week ago, there weren’t protocols in place for *any* of this. Well, now there are. And between the data we acquired from *Hightower* and the data from Major Kuehng’s drone... I think we got somethin’ to talk about. Roll the video, please.”

The screen switched to what was obviously the view from the aerostat. Holding station in the high upper atmosphere, aerostats like these were as close to space as humans had ever gotten on their own. The curvature of the earth was clearly visible, in a view that included the Gulf of Mexico to the left and the Pacific to the right. The land visible below was a deep green, overlaid with clouds.

A sudden, bright light occurred in the center of the screen. Piercingly bright, it rapidlycoalesced into a rolling cloud with a mushroom shape that quickly climbed into the sky.

“We don’t really know what this was,” Charley Lochart said, from his end of the table. “We do know that it occurred at the same time the ‘acquisition’ event happened here. An apparently enormous energy release occurred in a tightly confined area. Republic of Central America is calling it a ‘volcanic eruption’ in press releases and working to get ground crews into the area. But there seems to have been almost no damage... and there should have been.”

“Then there’s *this*,” Major Kuehng said from his end of the table. “Roll the drone footage, please.”

The screen switched to a treetop level view of a tropical rainforest. In the foreground: what looked like a Mayan temple. Not far from it, a familiar spindle shape floated above the trees. The camera panned away from the temple to what looked like a small mountain. The same bright flash, the same coalescing cloud–enormous from this viewpoint–then the camera seemed to shake violently before going dark.

"We had to use *Hightower* as a 'bounce' relay to get this," Kuehng said. "The drone survived the blast, actually, but I bet it was one helluva ride. We pulled the 'self-destruct' switch not long after that. No sense in letting *Los Centros* get our tech for free–particularly when it ain't supposed to be in their airspace in the first place.

"There's one last thing on this part of the agenda," Charley said. "Both *Hightower* and Major Kuehng's drone detected an object *leaving* the blast–an object *Hightower's* sensors tracked out of the atmosphere before it lost contact."

"If *Hightower's* sensors are that good," I said, "it seems to me that you should have been able to independently confirm at least *some* of the 'mystery disk' and 'ghost airship' data the Republic of California just agreed to share with you. Anything else I 'need to know,' General Bush?"

"I am *genuinely* going to miss you, Captain Cullen," Bush said. "Next time you see Hiram, you tell him I said you got another promotion or two comin'.

"Actually, *Hightower* does a pretty good job of trackin' stuff we can *see*. The problem is that a lot of these 'exotics' don't *want* to be seen, are pretty good at comin' and goin' as they please. Maybe 'Ghost Two' will give us a leg up on the problem–but that's Charley's business, not mine.

"There is one last thing we got for you for now... and you'll understand why we saved it for last. Sandy, how about rollin' that clip from the lab?"

* * * *

There was now an electric fence around the hangar, topped with razor wire. The sign at the gate read “HANGAR FIFTY-TWO. Red Devil One and above clearance ONLY.”

Saul chuckled. “They actually kept the name.”

“Texicans have a sense of humor in all things,” I said. “I have no idea what ‘Red Devil One’ clearance is... but I’m assuming we have it.”

As we approached the gatehouse, the Texas Ranger on duty broke into a broad grin. “Howdy, Saul! If you wanna cook some more hot dogs, we still got your grill stashed in the back.”

“We’re good,” Saul said.

Inside the hangar, a couple of technicians were scraping the silver paint from the floor and putting it in a bucket. “If they think they can figure out what happened from analyzing the paint,” Saul said, with a chuckle, “Good luck. It doesn’t work that way.”

The spindle-shaped object in the middle of the hangar was covered by a number of heavy tarps, all of which had been chained to iron rings in the floor.

“That happened quick,” Saul said.

“You were out for *days*,” I told him. “For a bit, it looked like you’d sustained actual brain damage. In any case, *all* of this is temporary. A permanent facility has already been approved.”

We walked past the covered ‘ghost airship.’ The far end of the hanger was closed off as well, this time by corrugated steel sheeting. The door in the middle of the partition was also steel, with a card reader lock.

“That’s new as well,” Saul said. “I assume the tank is still there?”

"The tank's the same. But there's a few other changes."

I swiped my badge through the card reader and led him in.

I had expected the sharp intake of breath, but not the chuckle.

"Yeah," Saul said. "You could say that."

I'd once seen Saul floating in that tube, undergoing a procedure that everyone involved admitted was basically torture. Before that, Saul and I had both seen the child-sized creature now floating in its center in another, similar tube in another place. That sight had driven him to an extreme stage of anxiety that had triggered an equally extreme reaction... but, apparently, that wasn't happening this time. Even so, the enormous black eyes still raised the small hairs on the back of my neck.

To the left of the Grey alien floated... an atrocity.

It looked like someone had placed a human being and a Grey alien in a blender. Same ashen skin, same enormous eyes–but the eyes were blue instead of black, even though they were equally unseeing. The thing had a bulbous, misshapen head with random wisps of blond hair, a frail body, and was just as much infiltrated with machinery as Ruhl Skattersmythe–the *same* machinery, according to Charley Hardin. Its right arm still seemed mostly human. Its right hand... grasped the hand of the alien creature floating next to it.

"So that's your friend 'Case,' right?"

"Yeah," Saul said. "The 'real' Colvin Case and *his* friend, 'Celeste.' What the hell is that other thing?"

That 'other thing' floated to the right of the Grey: a network of filaments that might've resembled a human nervous system, connected to something the size and shape of a walnut. Some of the filaments entangled the Grey's right hand... in about the place a left hand would be.

"According to Charley, it *was* your implant. I'm not an expert on these things, but it appears to be growing a brain and a nervous system."

"Do Charley or Ameryst have any theories on this?"

"None," I replied. "And Case isn't talking, right now. He says he's 'resting'."

"Is that *really* what he said?"

"No. Actually, he told us to fuck off and come back later. But after what he's done, he can have a couple of days off. You know there's a 'fail safe' on that tank, right?"

"I *thought* something looked different," Saul said. "How does that work?"

"Pretty simple, really. Take a look at the floor–see anything familiar?"

"The circle's still there. It looks like the guys scraping up paint intentionally left it."

"Very much so," I said. "If *anything*, physical or otherwise, enters or exits that circle without prior authorization, a million electron volts are getting fed through that tank."

"Do *they* know?"

"Absolutely."

* * * *

The screen went blank for a moment, then relit.

"We had to wash this through a *bunch* of filters," Sandy Lochart said. "Then we sent the data to Cali, so your folks at BSI could work on it as well. Magnified all to hell and slowed down, this is the last thing T.J.'s drone ever sent back."

Once again, we could see a small mountain peak–only now, not from a distance. A coppery, spindle-shaped object floated next to it, looking like a smaller version of 'Ghost One.'

Slowed down, the brilliant flash of light was clearly a fireball consuming the top of the mountain... which then coalesced into an orange column of smoke and flame.

And something else.

Darting from the source of destruction, something flew around the growing column–once, then twice, as the view zoomed in even closer.

"Assume I'm just an old country boy that don't know nothin'," Major Kuehng said, "Can someone *please* explain what the hell is *that*?

"I'm just guessing," Saul said. "But I think that might be the 'Demiurgos' that Ruhl keeps rattling on about."

A serpentine shape, maybe ten meters or so in length, shining in the fiery light as though made of gold. A few meters down from the snake-like head sprouted what looked like wings, also golden. Astride the serpent, just before the wings, a tall and naked woman.

Either her hair was the color of the red column of flame or took color from it. She was either laughing or screaming or both... I couldn't tell.

"*That's* what *Hightower* tracked into space?" Bush asked.

"It sure seems that way," Charley Hardin said.

****

“This is all going to be very interesting,” Saul said, taking a sip of his beer, “But I’m ready to go back to what’s left of my life in California. When does that airship arrive?”

Sanchez held up a bowl of roasted peanuts with an inquiring look. I shook my head, had a sip of my own beer. “Pretty soon,” I said. “But there’s a change of plans you need to be aware of.”

“What?” Saul asked. “Do the Texicans have another tank waiting for me?”

“Quite the opposite, actually. After some discussion, General Bush and I have decided to inform the Admiralty that you are temporarily remaining in Texas as a consultant.”

“Dammit, Kayce, you’re as high-handing as goddam Hiram Díaz–you *know* I want to go home!”

“You want to go back to your old life,” I told him, “or something like it–but that’s not going to happen. Even if they don’t put you on an operating table, neither BSI or the admiralty are ever going to just let you walk away.”

“So what, then? I just stay in Texas for the rest of my life?”

“No... but you aren’t getting on that airship with me. You’re going to be on a different itinerary.”

“Okay, Kayce–I *really* expected better, at least of you. What’s going on?”

“A couple of things. For starters, I asked Lindsay Lochardt to do some research after we found out this ‘Murphy’ guy was supposed to have been from Texas. Turns out, he existed in this ‘Texas’ as well–only he died a few decades ago... pretty much at around your age, after an auto accident.”

“And what does this have to do with me?”

I reached into my jacket pocket and handed him a folded piece of paper. “Here’s a photostat of his last driver’s license. Look familiar?”

Saul looked at it for a long time. “Yeah, just a bit,” he finally said. “What do you and Bush have in mind?”

From another pocket, I handed him a manila envelope. “That’s a current Republic of Texas passport in the name of ‘Miguel Estefan Alejandro Murphy’ with a photo that matches the one on your Republic of California Citizen’s ID and your birthdate. The corresponding record in Texas’ citizenship database shows a mailbox in Dallas as a permanent address, the same birthdate as your passport... and no date of death.

“There’s also a first class ticket to San Francisco for Miguel Murphy. Whether or not you use it is up to you.”

“What happens to ‘Saul Ellsberg’?” he asked.

“Nothing. But I *strongly* suggest that anyone who fits your general description who plans to set foot in San Francisco *anytime* soon should not be traveling with a passport bearing that name.”

“Isn’t this going to cause you problems?”

“Not really,” I said. “What becomes of ‘Saul Ellsberg,’ after I’m no longer in Texas, is hardly anything I’m going to be held responsible for–particularly after giving notice that I am leaving BSI and returning fulltime to teaching at the academy. Admiral Díaz is probably going to take some heat for hiring such a person in the first place... but the Admiral has decided to retire.”

“What about my back pay?”

"Whatever else might be said of Saul Ellsberg," I said, "at least he had the good sense to give his literary agent power of attorney prior to leaving the country."

He grinned sourly. "And I can count on Janice to remember that conversation... whether it ever really happened or not. What time is that first class flight to Frisco?"

"Early tomorrow," I told him. "I can order us some food, if you like."

"Yeah, maybe," he said. "So what, exactly, does 'Miguel Murphy' do for a living? I'm assuming he's not a writer."

"I believe he's some sort of consultant."

Saul snorted. "No doubt. It occurs to me that he might also be very possibly able to go places where 'Saul Ellsberg' might be less than welcome.

"But I'm sure that neither you, General Bush, nor Agent Lochardt ever gave a thought to that–and, of course, Hiram Díaz doesn't know *anything* about this... even if he wasn't retiring."

"Of *course* not."

He gave me a sudden hug I wasn't expecting. "I think you're right about my old life, Kayce. I'm not even sure it's *worth* going back to–even though I am for *damned* sure not staying here. I still wish I could've met Murphy... but I guess I don't really have to.

He gave me another hug, drained his beer and stood up. "Thanks, Kayce–thanks for *everything*."

## *two: murphy*

The beach was gray, the sky was gray, the water was gray. The dunes behind the beach were topped with dull brown beachgrass that was basically gray as well. The sound of the Pacific surf was oddly muted. There were no other sounds at all.

When the fog rolled out, that would change–at least the sky and the sea, at least for a little while.

The firepit on the beach-facing side of the deck is an iron cauldron, as wide as the width between the fingertips of one outreached open hand and the other. Etched into it are symbols that look like stars and galaxies, as well as runes and stuff that the old woman who runs the herb shop up the street calls 'enochian script.' It all reminds me of something... I just can't remember *what*.

After what could have been a *really* serious accident, I'd reassessed a lot of shit. I'd let grief and loneliness drive me into some really bad places. I'm not entirely sure I buy into what my therapist tells me, but the alternative is believing that the insane shit I woke up from is somehow *not* the product of some fairly massive trauma. Something seems weird about the timing... but that's true of a lot of things.

One of the things I had agreed with my therapist on was that I needed a change of scenery. Lucky for me, 'digital asset consulting' is one of those things you can do from *anywhere* with decent Internet.

"Throw on another log, old buddy," said a voice from the end of the deck. "There's some cold damp in that wind."

"So says the guy from Texas," I mocked, as I walked over to the woodpile. "You guys might want to pack it in before sunset, if you think *this* is cold."

"So says the guy from Texas who got here first and acts like he invented the place," he said, topping off a couple of wine glasses.

I'm not sure what had surprised me more–my old boss turning up in the Northwest or turning up married. I'd always thought of Colvin Case as a 'confirmed bachelor,' if you know what I mean... and pretty much married to the job in *any* case.

His new wife, Celeste, is a petite blonde woman of few words and large blue eyes that take in *everything*. They were sitting on the other side of the firepit in a couple of the beat-up old redwood adirondack chairs my buddy Travis favors, huddled under wool blankets, holding hands, sipping wine. Seeing them like that, it was hard to imagine they had not always been together.

I found an appropriate chunk of oak and added it to the fire.

Cape Disappointment isn't Portland, but Portland really isn't Portland anymore either–I'm far from the only one who decided to get out. I'd passed through here before, in what now seems another life. I'd liked the quietness, then–as well as the solitude.

About the time Case was trying to talk me into investing in a beachfront condo development, I found out another friend was looking for a place on the peninsula to open a brewpub.

Travis had always been my favorite bartender at the old Lyin' Lamb, as well as an astute judge of what to buy. The idea of him brewing his own beer within walking distance of where I was planning on living was too damned good not to make happen. The one condition of helping him open 'Lyin' Lamb II' had been the deck and the firepit–that, and making sure there would always be a good Cascadian Dark Ale on tap.

He'd agreed to it all–who *doesn't* like sitting in front of a fire, sipping a strong dark ale, and listening to the surf crash into the cape? Even better, he and his wife bought one of the condos when they went on the market.

Case's wife, Celeste, says she knows a lot of people who'd be interested if any other units get developed, but I don't know how the folks who'd already been living here would feel about that. They prefer the company of their own kind.

I'd wondered how it was going to work out when we sold a unit to an art dealer from San Francisco and her wife–again, Cape Disappointment is *not* Portland–but it turned out to be no big deal. The fact that Astor and Allie Luciel travel a lot probably helps. But they're great fun for my own little group when they're here. Allie keeps threatening to introduce me to her sister Evie... one of these days, I might even let her do it.

The highway isn't far from here, and there's another highway that forms a crossroad. If I wanted to, I could get my old motorcycle out of the shed and go anywhere in existence I wanted to... crossroads are magical that way.

But other forms of magic are more appealing to me.

I'm the unofficial master of the firepit. The craftsman who crafted the cauldron gave us a rod made of the same black iron. When I use it to stir up a good bed of coals, the symbols carved into the cauldron take light and the sparks swirling upward can look even more like even more stars and galaxies than the etched symbols in the pit–burning bright against the black, fogbound night.

The craftsman who crafted the cauldron gifted me a chalice as well, also wrought of black iron, also adorned with runes. I sip from it ale that is also dark as night, keeping company with my neighbors and tending the fire. None of us are *really* what we seem, but all of us welcome the shared illusion of an island of light, heat, and form amid the blackness and the sound of nearby endless sea.

For me, that cauldron holds the totality of memories, dreams, and hopes. Everything that ever was, ever will or could be... I can imagine as worlds within the crucible's starlike swirling sparks.

For all I know, I merely awaken to a dream from other dreams. For all I know, the other lives and other faces I remember when I think I've awakened exist in that swirl of sparks. For all I know... the stars I see when the nights are clear are just sparks swirling in some other cauldron.

Or maybe the same one.

We talk, my neighbors and I, sometimes long into the night... sharing that totality, sharing the welcome peace–even if it's temporary–of a crucible of light, warmth, and order. But eventually there comes time to empty the chalice into the cauldron, extinguish the last dying embers, and venture out to whatever awaits in the darkness.

I think that time is *now*, my friend. I'm glad you could join us, hope you had fun as well. Thank you for talking to me.

Stay safe... have a nice walk home.

# Afterword

The problem with writing as a form of therapy is that the need for therapy and the desire to write do not always align.

The first of these books, *Morningstar*, was started in order to find something to do with my free time other than self-medicate. I eventually realized that 'Murphy' had been created so he could experience a closure I knew I would never have. Along the way, I realized that his demiurgic drinking buddy existed to put both Murphy and me in our respective places. If a being as old as time could endure through millions of years of abandonment and loneliness, surely we mere mortals could find a way past our own pain and disappointment… right?

The following book, *Dawn Matter*, is admittedly a bit of a mess. This is common with sequels to books that were never intended to have sequels. But it is a *fun* mess, and it echoes the fun I had discovered in writing once the need for therapy was not so great. Finding an excuse to revisit Murphy wasn't easy, but I found one. Putting him in a place where I could tell more stories about him was easier. I just took a long look at everything wrong with my own universe… and created one I liked better.

*Ordo Seclorem* and *Crucible Luciferum* both wound up going on hold for a period of roughly four years. Career demands lessened my available free time, the prospect of living in a decent country diminished the need for therapy. Without going into unnecessary detail… let's just say that *both* of these circumstances have altered.

I go back and forth on the need to further explore my little pocket universe where corporatist acquiescence to tinpot dictators extends no further west than the Mississippi River, 'Texicans' really *are* badasses, and there really is a 'Federation' that guarantees peace and prosperity to those who choose to be part of a civilized world–at least those parts that include Pacific beachfront property. Which, not too coincidentally, are about the only parts of *this* world I continue to really care about.

On the one hand, this story is pretty much told. The current trend of fictional narratives that explain *everything* is not one that interests me. Boba Fett doesn't really need a back story, other than to generate more coin for the megacorp that owns him as intellectual property (a contradiction of terms, if there ever *was* one).

On the other hand, it's kind of a *nice* little pocket universe. It beats the hell out of the one I have to wake up in. As both my free time and desire for something therapeutic to do with it increases... I can't really rule it out.

Cheers and Peace,

AJC

# About the Author

A.J. Curry is a writer with interests including history, fantasy, science fiction, and the occult-in no particular order, and not excluding other interests as well. Their preferred beverage is a dirty martini with pepper-infused vodka.

# About the Publisher

Rose City Digital is a Portland-based boutique digital agency offering a wide range of creative and technical consulting services. RCD Press is their publishing consultancy, providing services and assistance to Pacific Northwest self-published authors.

For more information, visit https://rosecity.digital.

# Crucible Luciferum



Published 2026 by

RCD Press, Portland, OR



979-8-9985988-7-6

Paperback

www.ingramcontent.com/pod-product-compliance
Lightning Source LLC
LaVergne TN
LVHW020719110826
845149LV00012B/2329

* 9 7 9 8 9 9 8 5 9 8 8 7 6 *